Left Behind

by

Vi Keeland & Dylan Scott

"Stars can't shine without a little darkness."

— *Unknown*

Left Behind

ISBN-13: 9781682304259

Edited by: Caitlin Alexander
Cover model: Siselee Maughan
Cover designer: Sommer Stein, Perfect Pear Creative
Photographer: Christie Q. Photography
Interior layout: Deena Rae @ E-BookBuilders www.e-bookbuilders.com

Contents

To my remarkable husband— I wish I had met you sooner
so I could love you longer.

– *Dylan*

.

~~To my two sweet daughters~~

~~Dedicated to my well behaved children~~

~~For my girls, for never fighting~~

~~To my daughters, who never slam doors~~

~~Sugar and spice and everything nice, that's what little girls are made of~~

~~For not blasting your music while I'm trying to write~~

~~Presented to my children who always listen~~

For Grace and Sarah, I love you tons.

- Vi

Chapter 1

Nikki—

Brookside, Texas

I stand in the parking lot alone, rain pelts down on me so hard it should sting my fair skin, but I feel no pain. The navy sundress I'm wearing, the one and only dress I own, is soaked through, clinging tightly against my body. Squeezing my eyes shut, I pray to a god I'm not sure I believe in anymore, begging him to take the image that was just seared into my brain from my memory. But it's no use. Closing my eyes only makes the visual of her lying there even more vivid. I force them back open to chase what I see away, but it doesn't work.

My body begins to shake, sobs racking through me even before my tears begin to fall. It's the first time I've cried since it happened. Time goes by, but I have no idea how long I stand there letting days of pent-up emotions wash over me. Eventually, the heavy rain begins to dwindle, my tears following its lead.

Headlights catch my attention in the distance, slowing before turning into the dimly lit parking lot. Ducking behind a nearby tree, I have no idea why I'm hiding. I only know I don't want to see whoever it is. I peek my head out from behind the tall oak to catch a glimpse of the stranger. A woman parks, fixes her hair in the rearview mirror, and eventually gets out of the car. For a long moment, she stands motionless, looking at the words above the tall double doors.

Minutes later, a second car pulls in. This one I'm all too familiar with. Exiting her car, Ms. Evans spares no moment for reflection. She strides to the door, opens it and disappears inside without the blink of an eye. I've had lots of social workers over the years, but this one…she's the worst of them all. *I hate her.* Watching her stroll so casually into my mother's funeral reminds me of all the months she kept us apart. Time we could have spent together. Time I can't get back now.

The sadness and tears gone, anger overtakes me. My limp body goes rigid, fists ball tightly at my sides. *I hate her. So damn much.* Feeling like a pot full of boiling water, the lid about to come flying off because the steam needs to escape, I search the ground for something to throw. Anything. Finding a muddy rock, I hurl it towards the car that took me away so many times. It clunks when it connects with the car, but the sound doesn't satisfy me. So I find another and this time I wind up before I heave the heavy stone from my trembling hand. A loud shatter rings through the still parking lot. A hundred tiny pieces of glass fall to the ground as the alarm begins to sound. Oddly, the noise brings me peace.

I turn, feeling more satisfied than I have in days, water still dripping from everywhere on my body, and slowly walk towards home.

Chapter 2

Zack—

Long Beach, California

I remember the first time I laid eyes on Emily Bennett. Her family had just moved in across the street. The long white moving truck took up almost half of our block. I was sitting in my room on the second floor, peeking out the window. Most of the stuff I saw them unload looked like my family's stuff...expensive area rugs, antique furniture— all junk I wasn't allowed near. Stuff that looked boring as hell to a nine-year-old.

I was quickly growing uninterested in my spying, until something bright yellow caught my eye coming out of the never-ending truck. Twenty-six inches of gleaming chrome and bright canary-yellow high-gloss paint. *No way.* My mouth watered at the sight of the Schwinn Twin Back IV Racer I'd had my eye on for the last two months. I'm not sure if I was more excited to finally have a boy on my block to play with or that I might get to ride the new kid's bike. I darted down the stairs two at a time, ripped open the screen door so fast it nearly came off the hinges, and raced across the street, completely ignoring my mother screaming at me to put shoes on. And pants. Yeah, in all my excitement, I ran out in my underwear. Nine years old and my damn mother was still buying me Batman briefs. The memory of running straight into the new neighbor, only to find out the new *boy* was a *girl*, seems like a lifetime ago.

Emily and I have been inseparable ever since. She let me ride the Schwinn the very first day I met her. Right after I put my pants on and my mother forced me to politely introduce myself to Emily's parents— a very nice but serious couple who seemed a lot older and not quite as happy as my mom and dad.

I think I fell in love with Emily before I even understood what *falling in love* meant. When I was ten and my team lost the pee wee superbowl, Emily was right there in her cheerleading outfit, gushing over how I almost won the game for the whole team. And the next year, when my team won, Emily screamed and cheered louder than anyone. That was Emily— my biggest cheerleader, proud of every move I ever made and madly in love with me. How could a guy not love that?

But over the last couple of years a lot has changed. Emily has changed. Sometimes I don't recognize the Emily from the yellow Schwinn. As I watch that same little girl, now all grown up, saunter to our table I search her eyes for a sign of the Emily she used to be. I'm sad when I can't find her.

She's still as beautiful as ever though. Emily tosses her hair. Long, blonde, and straight at the top, with curls starting midway down her back, it looks like she spent hours getting ready just to come to school. Knowing Emily, she probably did.

"Ready to go, Batman?" Emily returns to our lunch table after making her daily social rounds. Eight years later and she's still torturing me about that day. Only, these days, she knows what I really have on underneath, dark grey Calvin Klein boxer briefs. The same kind she likes to grind her half naked body against a few times a week, but still won't let me take off.

"Go without me. I'm gonna go talk to Allison Parker. She's my partner for our English project." I know my response won't sit well with Emily, but I'm almost at the point of not giving a shit anymore.

"Really, Zack? Again? If I didn't know better, I'd start to think you and the little nerd girl had something going on." She knows Allison and I are just friends, that's not what she's really pissed about. All of her stuck-up friends meet in the courtyard every day after they're done eating, and god forbid she doesn't have me to tote around. Most days she doesn't even talk to me anymore, but she hangs on to me like we're goddamn connected at the hip.

"You won't even notice I'm not there." I stand and grab my books from the table, silently marking the end of the conversation. For me, anyway.

"Of course I will, and so will everyone else," she whines, reaching for my hand.

And there's the real reason that I'm getting bitched at for wanting to work on my English project. The captain of the cheerleading squad *must* be seen with the captain of the football team. The earth might tilt off its axis if all isn't picture perfect in Emily's world. But I'm a master at fixing my wrongs with Emily Bennett, so I slam my books down on the table loudly, making sure all eyes are on us. Then I wrap my arms around her tiny waist and pull her close, making it so she has to tilt her pretty little head up to look at me. Sealing my mouth over hers, I kiss her long and hard.

She'll pretend to be pissed at my little public display of affection, but she won't be. She loves every damn minute of the attention. And the more girls who sigh as she strolls by, the better the treatment I'll get when I see her again after school.

Nikki—

Brookside, Texas

The morning sun shining through the trees does nothing to lift my mood. After tossing and turning all night, I was more exhausted when I climbed out of bed than when I'd crawled into it.

Sleep deprivation leaves me edgy and I jump when my cell rings. "I haven't leaped out a window, Ashley," I yell as I hit the speaker button on the phone, halting my cleaning of Mom's dresser drawers. She means well, but she called four times already and it's only 11 a.m. "Shouldn't you be in math class?"

"I'm smart enough. Besides, I'll get by in life on my charm alone," she says sarcastically. "Calculus is for the dim witted."

"Really? I always thought Calculus was for smart kids."

"Nah. They just tell that to the kids with no personality so they don't hop out a window. We tell them they're bright, but what it really means is *you're boring as shit so you have to work twice as hard.*"

"You do know people tell me I'm *bright*, right?"

7

"That's okay, stick with me, I'll dumb you down." She pauses. "I only have English and gym left, thought I'd cut out and keep you company this afternoon."

Surprisingly, I'm able to talk Ash out of cutting class, I know she wants to see for herself that I'm okay. That's why I didn't mention I found out I'll be moving next week. Ms. Evans handed me the news this morning. Foster care. Again. Ashley's mom agreed to keep me temporarily, but her trailer has less room than mine.

My frequent stints in foster care whenever Mom was hospitalized were usually short lived. I knew they were only temporary. But I still have almost a full year until I turn eighteen and I don't even want to think about living with strangers for all that time. I can't imagine surviving without Mom *and* Ashley.

Ashley Mason has been my best friend for four years. It's the longest I've ever had a best friend. Actually, it's the longest I've had *any* friend. We met in Mr. Carson's English class. We had just started *To Kill a Mockingbird* when I transferred into Brookside. I'm the geek who reads two books a week and has every English assignment done before it's due. Ashley is the other kind of girl. The kind who reads Spark Notes and despises any book that doesn't have pictures. Some people just hate to read, Ashley is their queen. She couldn't fathom that I'd already read *To Kill a Mockingbird* because I wanted to. Our obvious differences are what attracted us to each other. Ashley needed help and I gave help. It's who I am. I guess all those years of taking care of Mom made it second nature for me.

I toss my phone on the bed and take a deep breath looking around. Who will I take care of now?

Notebooks filled with rambling thoughts.

Random newspaper articles folded into tiny squares.

Hundreds of empty pills bottles.

I'm grateful Ashley decided to stay in school; it gave me some time to finish cleaning out Mom's drawers without having to explain anything. I know Ash won't judge us. But some of the stuff I sorted through this morning has no explanation. Ashley knows all about Mom. She's one of the few people who did. Mom's diabetes wasn't a secret— it was ultimately what took her life. But hardly anyone knew about her mental illness. It wasn't something that was easy to explain. Most kids don't even know what Bipolar Disorder is, let alone how to take care of a mother battling its demons each day. It was just easier not to bring anyone home. Except Ashley. She's seen it all. Especially, the last few rough weeks…Mom's disease was all about bad days and good days. But we hadn't had any good days in a while. A really, really long while.

I look around the small trailer Mom and I shared the last four years. As always, my stuff is ready to go— easy to move. I never trusted permanency any more than Mom did. We had a silent understanding that my belongings would stay in the heavy cardboard boxes I kept organized like drawers. Even when Mom and I lived in a furnished place with real dressers, I never used one.

It's Mom's things that need to be organized and sorted through. It's not a chore I'm comfortable with. Mom always kind of kept her things private. Even though she's gone, I still feel like I'm doing something wrong going through her things.

The back of Mom's drawer is where she keeps her jewelry box. I'm not sure why she always hid it, neither of us ever owned anything of value. I open the pink tattered box; the familiar ballerina pops up to greet me and suddenly I'm six and sneaking into Mom's bedroom when she's not home. I'd wind and wind the music box, watching the little plastic ballerina twirl around to the music and trying to imitate her pose. "You can hardly walk and chew gum at the same time," Mom said, laughing, when I asked her if I could sign up for ballet lessons. Never mind that we couldn't have afforded it.

I can't help myself. I wind the key at the back of the box tightly, and as the music pings, the first real smile I've felt in weeks visits my face.

Two long strands of metallic beads wrapped around my neck, I hum the ballerina's song as I slip cheap costume jewelry rings onto every finger. The silver one with the dark purple stone changes colors. I remember Mom telling me it was her mood ring; that it could see how she felt inside. Dark green meant sad, red meant happy. I'd always thought she was teasing me. But staring intently at my finger, I watch as the dark purple turns to green.

"You playing dress up without me?"

Startled, I jump from the bed, sending the jewelry box sailing across the room, the contents emptying all over the place as the box slams into the wall.

"Ashley! You scared the crap out of me!"

She grins. "I'm sorry. You didn't answer when I knocked, so I let myself in. Nice safety precaution by the way, leaving the front door wide open so any strange person can walk in."

"And apparently they did." I drop to my hands and knees in search of Mom's jewelry, now strewn all over her tiny bedroom. It's not valuable measured in terms of money, but the junk is priceless to me.

"You weren't answering my calls." Ashley's worry is in her voice and written on her face. I look up, finding the tips of her jet black hair have been dyed violet since only last night. So Ashley. I'm really going to miss her.

"Sorry, Ash. I just needed some time to go through Mom's things." I reach down to grab the music box from the floor where it crash landed and lift it, turning it upright, but the tray glued to the bottom dislodges and tumbles to the floor in the process. Two tiny plastic strips that must have been tucked between the tray and the bottom of the music box fall, landing at my feet.

Ashley picks them up, squinting at the faint words typed on the small pink strips of plastic. "Isn't your birthday February 14th?"

"Yes, you know it is. Remember, you bought me that big chocolate Valentine's Day heart and wrapped it in birthday paper? I always get ripped off on my birthday," I tease. But something in Ashley's face wipes the smile off mine. Taking the strips from her hand, I read the words that have caused her cheery pink face to drain of all its color. One bracelet reads: *Twin A, 2/14/97, Mother: Carla Fallon.* The second bracelet reads: *Twin B, 2/14/97, Mother: Carla Fallon.*

Chapter 4

Zack—

Long Beach, California

Saturday mornings are my favorite times with Emily. Lunging to stretch my calves, I watch as she walks across the street dressed in her running gear. No makeup, a headband pulling her hair back into a simple ponytail, she looks young and beautiful. More like the girl I fell in love with than the one she's become lately. Somehow, the casualness of her appearance seeps into her attitude, making her lose the air of superiority that seems to have gotten worse the last few months.

"Morning." She smiles broad and happy, stretching up on her tippy toes as she kisses my cheek.

"Someone got up on the right side of the bed this morning." I switch to the other leg, lunging to complete my pre-run stretch.

"What is there not to be happy about?" I'm in total agreement, but curious as to what makes her realize it for herself this morning.

Beginning her own stretches, Emily spreads her legs, leaning over dramatically, placing both palms on the ground in front of her. Her ass perfectly positioned in front of me. Definitely intentional, but who am I to complain with such a great view. "I agree. In fact, I'm feeling happier by the minute." I swat her ass. She giggles like a little girl.

"You wanna do the loop through town to the library and back, or head for the track at the school this morning?" We've been running together Saturday mornings since middle school. Sometimes I think it's the only time I enjoy with Emily anymore. And maybe the times her parents go out for a few hours and I sneak over, but that always starts well and ends with me frustrated.

"Loop." She puts one hot pink ear bud in, leaving the other dangling. "Race you to old man Wilkins' house? Loser buys lunch." Emily takes off before I can even respond.

Wilkins' house is two blocks away, but they're long blocks. I let her lead for about a block and a half. Then I blow past her, just as she starts to smell victory in the near distance. Neither one of us likes to lose at anything, it's one of the few things we have in common anymore. But also one of the things that gets in our way.

"You cheated." Face flushed, leaning over with both hands on her knees as she tries to catch her breath, Emily frowns.

"How can I cheat? It's a race and you took off before me. It's not like I got in the car and drove here when you weren't looking."

"You made me think I was going to win."

"So?"

"So, that's cheating."

"That's not cheating, that's playing with you."

"Playing with me?" She stands, hands on her hips.

"Yep." I lean down and kiss her chastely. She's still out of breath, but I can see she's trying not to let it show. I'm not winded at all.

"Well, let's see if you'll get to *play with me* tonight, then."

"That sounds like a challenge." Taking a step into her personal space, I look down at her, trying my best to intimidate her. But it only makes her feistier.

"Maybe if you'd let me win once in a while, I'd let you win."

We spend two hours running together and then I buy her lunch, even though she lost the bet. I'm not even sure why I agree to her bets, because even when I win, she doesn't lose.

She pushes half her salad around on her plate with her fork. "My parents are going out of town next Saturday night for a convention."

"Oh yeah? You staying with Blair?"

"I was thinking I'd tell my parents I was staying with Blair, but we could stay at my house. Have the whole night together." Emily bites her bottom lip, it's her nervous tell. Ever since we were kids I could always tell when she was scared, even though she put up a brave front most of the time.

"Maybe you can tell your parents you're staying at Keller's house after the bonfire down at the beach. By the time we get home, your parents will be asleep and they won't even notice us slip back into my house."

I know what she's telling me— damn, we've even argued about it a few times over the last year. It feels like I've been waiting forever. But now that she's offering it to me, I feel guilty even thinking about taking it from her unless she's ready.

"We don't have to, Em." Reaching out, I slip her hand into mine on top of the table. "I'll wait, if you're not ready." I may freaking explode, but I'll wait.

"I want to."

"You sure?"

She leans in, her voice low, "I went on the pill last month. I'm ready."

Jesus, I can't believe it's finally gonna happen. Just thinking about it, I'm glad I'm sitting so the whole diner can't see the strain at the crotch of my pants.

Maybe I was letting my pent-up frustration out on Emily the last few months and it was affecting our relationship. Because everything seems to have gotten lighter, more carefree. Together we feel more like the old Zack and Em than we have in years.

I close Emily's door and walk around to my side of the car. She scoots close to me, resting her hand on my lap affectionately. "Pretty soon I'll be driving your ass to the movies."

I turn the key in the ignition and the engine on my dad's restored sixty-eight Charger comes to life. I still can't believe he lets me take this thing. "Driver pays for the movie, you know," I tease.

"I didn't know there were rules."

"Yep. Lots of 'em. You get a typed list mailed to you with your license. You know, assuming you pass your road test."

"You don't think I'm a good driver?" Emily's hand flies to her chest in a feigned, overdramatic pose.

"Men are better drivers." I shrug.

She laughs. "What are you talking about?"

"It's a known fact."

"Known to whom?"

"Everyone."

"It's not known to me."

"That's because you don't have your license yet. Those facts come in the same envelope with the rules."

I pull up to the movie theatre. A gaggle of her girlfriends wave as I park. "They're all coming to the movie?"

"They're all my besties."

"How can you have so many besties? You do know the term best refers to the most excellent *one*, right?" I tease, only half joking.

"You and your rules." Emily checks her makeup for the third time in just the short distance to the theatre.

It takes less than five minutes for me to lose the Emily I was really enjoying today once she surrounds herself with her friends. I stop to say hello to two guys from my Spanish class and Emily rolls her eyes at me. I spend the movie missing the feel of her hand on my lap since she's sitting between her two besties whispering. But the distance growing between us is far more than physical.

Chapter 5

Nikki—

Brookside, Texas

I wake in the clothes I wore yesterday. My head pounding and mind swirling, morning brings me no more clarity than yesterday. Except now I'm sober. At least I think I am. Daring to crack one eye open, my line of sight like a magnet to metal, the first thing I see in my cloudy vision is the tiny pink wristbands. I barely make it to the bathroom before emptying the contents of my stomach.

My dry heaving and retching wakes Ashley from her slumber, and she comes to check on me. She looks almost as bad as I feel.

"What the hell did we drink?" Ash wets an old facecloth and folds it over her head, laying her body across the cool tiled bathroom floor next to where I sit hugging the porcelain bowl.

Unable to lift my head to look at her, I try to remember. There was vodka. Not much, just three little mini bottles, the kind they give out on airplanes. Mom had them displayed on a shelf behind a plate painted with a picture of some old singer. I remember us drinking those…but I'm foggy what came after.

"We drank the little vodka bottles."

Groaning, Ashley chimes in, "And then the Gin."

"Gin?" Vaguely, I recall a deep green glass bottle. "Green bottle?"

"Yep."

"How much did we drink?"

"All of it. Then you smashed it outside against the side of the trailer."

"I did?" I'm shocked I can't remember it, not shocked at my actions.

"Yep. You were screaming pretty loud too."

Drinking is a favorite past-time in our trailer park, but it's not something Ash and I ever got into. Concern about getting caught enters my brain— most likely for the first time. Not much stays a secret in our little community. "Does your mom know?"

"I don't think so."

"How did you get her to let you sleep here?"

"I told her we were going to church and for a run and you shouldn't be alone after."

"Church?" I arch one eyebrow, but she can't see it because my head is still dangling over the toilet bowel. I'm not sure if the thought of Ashley in church or her joining me on one of my daily five-mile runs is less believable.

"It was that or go home, and I was afraid to leave you alone." Ashley's voice drops lower, almost a whisper. "I can't believe you might have a sister."

Hours later, my hangover is finally at bay from a double dose of Tylenol and a gallon of water. But looking around the room makes me feel queasy again, only this time it has nothing to do with alcohol.

All of my worldly belongings fit into eight boxes— my usual seven, and one new box from the grocery store packed with Mom's things I want to keep. Seventeen years of living and that's what I've managed to collect along the way. And one of the boxes is almost completely packed with books. As I tape up the last box, tires on the gravel driveway at the side of our trailer alerts me to a visitor. Peering out the kitchen window confirms the visitor isn't a welcome one. Evil Evans.

She knocks on the screen door frame, even though the inside door is wide open and she can clearly see me standing less than five feet away.

"Come in." I don't even stop what I'm doing to look up at her.

"How are you doing today, Nikki?" There's zero warmth in her voice. Aren't people who work with children supposed to be warm and comforting? This woman's more like the ice queen.

"What do you want? I thought I had until tomorrow."

"I came to give you something." I look to her, but she doesn't immediately move to take anything out. Instead, she forces me to make eye contact if I want to know what she's here to deliver. I wait, holding her stare.

"Your mother gave me something a few weeks ago. She asked me to give it to you after she was gone. I wanted to give you a few days to grieve before I brought it by."

Ms. Evans opens her bulging briefcase, slips out an envelope and holds it up. Mom's handwriting is on the outside. There's an ache in my chest, I fight the urge to reach up and clutch at it. "Did you read it?"

"No, I did not." Her monotone voice matches her drab gray suit.

"Give it to me." I put out my hand, my eyes never leaving hers. I won't back down to this horrible woman. She can't take me away from Mom since she's already gone. I stare at her expressionless face, not letting her see the emotion hidden behind a mask. Eventually she hands it over.

"I'll be back tomorrow. About noon?"

"Whatever." I turn my back and walk into the back bedroom, slamming the door behind me. I wait until I hear her car pull away before I tear open the envelope.

Seeing Mom's handwriting brings tears before I even begin to read her words.

Dear Nikki,

I know you're probably mad I'm gone. But being mad is good sometimes. It makes you keep your guard up. The world is filled with people you can't trust. They cloak themselves in good, but it only masks the bad underneath. You need to pay attention, find out who's really hiding underneath.

It takes only the first few sentences in the letter for me to know she wrote it during one of her dark periods. The days she refused to take her medicine. Sometimes the side effects from all of her different pills were worse than her condition itself. It left her exhausted, unable to get out of bed for days, sometimes even weeks at a time. Eventually, she'd stop taking the meds. The dark period that followed usually lasted a few weeks. At first it wasn't bad. But with each day off her medication, she'd become more and more paranoid. When I was younger, I thought it was true, that people really were out to get us. I constantly checked over my shoulder, like Mom did.

There are so many things that I should have told you. Things I kept from you because I needed to protect you. I didn't want them to separate us. I love you, Baby Girl. To the moon and back, just like the book I used to read you. Only more. Lots more. So all of the secrets I kept, I kept for us. Because we were stronger together than apart.

But now you're alone. So the truth needs to come out. I'm sorry to have kept it from you all these years. I don't know any other way to tell you. I wish there was an easier way.

Nikki, you have a fraternal twin sister. And an aunt too. Neither one of us is an only child. Although, in our hearts, we always will be.

Your sister was sick. I couldn't take care of her and take care of us. So your aunt made arrangements for us. She had the other baby adopted.

On your first birthday, I called your aunt to see if she could find out how your sister was. She said the baby left the hospital healthy and she didn't know more. She may have been lying, because they were listening. So I hung up fast so they couldn't trace the call and I never called her again. She vowed to keep the adoption a secret because the adoptive parents begged her to. They never plan to tell your sister she isn't their real child. I'm sorry I'm not there with you now. I hate to leave you all

23

alone. No one should be alone in the world. That's why I'm telling you about your aunt. Her name is Claire Nichols. She has means and will help you if you ask. But be careful. She'll stop at nothing to keep the secret of your sister from being exposed.

I'll love you always. To the moon and back.

Mom

By the time I'm done reading, some of the inked words are blurred from my tears. Clenching her letters tightly against my chest, I curl up on the bed and cry myself to sleep, repeating the words over and over. *To the moon and back, Mom. To the moon and back.*

The next afternoon, I freeze when I hear the knock on the trailer door. I'd rehearsed what I was going to say to Evil Evans all night, but now the words have left me. I barely eke out a "Come in." It's pretty ironic that I'm about to ask her for help, when all I wanted before was for her to leave me alone.

"Ready, Nikki?" We make eye contact, but I quickly look away, steadying myself with a deep breath.

"Ms. Evans, I need your help." I wrap my hands around my stomach— the words actually caused physical pain when I said them.

It's the first time I've ever seen her speechless.

"It's about the letter from my mom." My eyes well up with tears. "I have an aunt," I blurt out. "Her name is Claire Nichols. I need to find her. I really need to find her. Will you please help me?" I was up half the night searching the internet, there's more than four thousand people with my aunt's name. Ms. Evans could search records…maybe even hire an investigator.

She listens to me explain what I want her to do. "Nikki— "

"Please, Ms. Evans, please. Don't take me anywhere yet. Just try to find her first. Please. She's my only family."

I sense her mentally paging through her caseload, deciding if I'm worthy. "It may not be as easy to find her as you think." She sighs and looks toward the ceiling. Eventually she reluctantly agrees. "You can't stay here. I'll have to talk to Ashley's mom about keeping you a few more days. If she can't"— the warning in her voice is clear— "you'll have to go to the foster family tonight."

I don't tell Ms. Evans about my sister. *My sister.* After Evans leaves, I say the words aloud to myself to see how it sounds. "My sister." After seventeen years, how can someone have a sister?

I hate to cry. Telling Ash about Mom's letter would most definitely open the floodgates. So instead, I just hand her the envelope and let her read the whole crazy story for herself. As she finishes reading, *Ashley* starts to cry. I can't hold back my tears when I see hers. We hug, clinging to each other tightly.

It takes a little coaxing. Ashley actually begs her mom to let me stay with them for a little while longer. It's not that her mom doesn't like me, but she does dislike an extra body in their small trailer, five kids cramp things enough. But Ashley convinces her and she reluctantly calls Ms. Evans to tell her I can stay.

"Mother of the year said you have a week. Generous, huh?" Ashley says as we walk to get some of my clothes.

"At least she's letting me stay." I shrug.

"Well, if we run out of time, I guess we'll just cut your hair into a mullet, glue on a scraggly mustache, and stuff a quarter keg beer belly into a red flannel. She'll find room for you then. Hell, she'll have the rest of her spawn calling you Uncle within a few days.

I laugh. Her depiction is a bit overly dramatic, but it's not that far off. "What happened to *Uncle* Kenny?"

"You mean *Uncle* Joe. *Uncle* Kenny was last month."

"That's right, I forgot you got a new Uncle."

"Don't bother remembering, he went out for milk and never came back." I look at Ashley in disbelief. "No, really. He *literally* went for milk. Mom gave him twenty bucks and he never came back."

I shake my head. "She's too nice."

"Sure." Ashley looks at me like I'm crazy. "We'll go with that."

"Honestly, I'm grateful she's letting me stay. I wouldn't last too long with anyone else."

"What choice do you have?"

"I don't know. I have a little money stashed away. I'm getting out of here, with or without Evans' help."

Chapter 6

Zack—

Long Beach, California

After Emily told me she was ready last weekend, I'd thought that maybe finally doing it would bring us closer together. But if this week is any indication of things to come, I'm starting to question if sleeping with Emily is even a good idea. Her usual bossiness has hit a new level of extreme this week. I secretly wonder if she thinks she can get away with anything now, because she holds the looming sex card over my head. She's been treating me like a dog with a bone held just out of his reach. Only pretty soon this dog may bite her and go find a nicer owner. It would be pretty ironic if I wound up turning her down in the end, after the last year of practically begging.

"Fine. Fine. Just stop yelling at me. I'll drive you home after practice and then come back to the library."

"Do you know how it looks when you hang out with *them* in public?" The way her lip twists up in a snarl makes her beautiful face turn ugly.

"Yeah. It *looks* like I have real friends, ones that aren't even more plastic than their credit cards," I shoot back, my voice laced with contempt I no longer try to hide.

Eyes wide, she has the audacity to look appalled. "My friends are not plastic!"

"I have to get to class." I open the door leading inside from the now empty courtyard. Everyone's already gone and I'm going to be late for English. I hold the door open and speak without turning back to face her, "You coming or not?"

Emily huffs, but stomps through the door. God forbid she be caught in the courtyard alone.

I sit in English class staring at Mr. Hartley, but I don't hear a word he says. My head is so jumbled, wondering where Emily and I veered off course to wind up in such different places. For the last eight years, we've always been Zack and Em. I don't think I ever really gave any thought to dating anyone else, everyone always just assumed Emily and I would wind up together, including me. But I'm not sure I can do it anymore. Some days, I barely recognize who she is; she's changed so much.

I used to think her attitude was part of her insecurity, putting other people down made her feel better about herself. On the outside, everyone sees a beautiful girl, full of confidence, fearless. Only I know the truth. She was criticized for years.

When we were younger, Emily hated her mother's fixation on social status. I remember one time, when we were ten or eleven, we rode our bikes to the park the day after a heavy rainstorm. The dirt under the swings had turned into thick, squishy mud. We spent hours chasing each other, tossing handfuls of mud until the only white visible was the whites of our eyes. We had the greatest day; neither of us could stop smiling. Until Mrs. Bennett caught sight of

28

us. She freaked out, worried what people might think if they saw her daughter covered in dirt.

For years Emily complained about her mother's obsessiveness over how things looked. How *she* looked. But then, a little at a time, she started to become the very thing she despised. The criticized became the critic. I know it's not really her fault. So for a long time, I put up with Emily putting people down, with no one ever being good enough, because that's all that she's ever known. But I'm tired of making excuses about who she's become to people…making excuses to myself.

"You okay?" Allie Parker breaks me out of deep thought. I look around, finding the class half empty. Guess I didn't hear the bell ring.

"Uh…yeah. I'm just tired today. Coach has us doing extra practice time with the game coming up." It's not a lie. The whole team has been putting in extra time, although physically I'm not tired at all.

"I can cover your part of the project. Why don't you go home and get some sleep?" Allie offers, a sweet smile on her face. She really is pretty. How have I never noticed it before? Dark hair, pale skin, green eyes with a hint of grey in them. The color is really unusual and I find myself staring to get a better look.

"You okay?" Allie tilts her head to the side, her smile fading to a look of concern. I force myself to snap out of it.

"Sorry. Yeah, I'm good. I'll meet you at the library after practice."

"Okay. But if you change your mind…we'll cover it. No worries."

Cheerleading practice ended before football practice today and, as usual, Emily is waiting for me outside of the locker room. I'm not sure what I expected after the scene in the courtyard a few hours ago, but she takes my hand and starts walking and talking as if nothing even happened.

"How long do you think you'll be at the library tonight?" she says, as though the subject hadn't sparked a heated argument only a short while ago.

"I have no idea, why?"

"My parents are going out to dinner with the Schumers tonight, they won't be back until late. Thought maybe you could stop over and help me with a few things." She turns and walks backward, still holding my hand. Her hips sway with each step. I don't ask what she needs help with, yet she continues anyway. "Like taking off my bra…rubbing night cream into my skin…," Emily trails off, allowing my brain to fill in the rest.

A year ago, I would have jumped at the chance, but my head just isn't lined up with the rest of my body that responds to her invitation without thinking. "Let me see how late we get done."

I drop her off and head back to the library. Being around her could give a guy whiplash. One minute she's hot, the next she's cold. Something about it seems more off than the usual mood swings I've come to accept as part of the charm that is Emily Bennett. Her highs are just higher these days and her lows are lower.

Allie and our two other English project partners are at the library working by the time I arrive. They're so easy to be around, it's a nice change to spend time with people who actually enjoy reading a book. Even if Emily had fun doing any of her homework, she'd never admit it for fear the cool police might catch her and kick her out of the elite club. The one she's the president and poster child for these days.

"Thank god, you're here. Allie and Cory want to do our project based on *The Scarlet Letter*. I need you on my side, dude." Keller Daughtry looks desperate for some testosterone to join him in the fight.

Our project is to read a book that is considered adult lit, pull out the conflicts and resolution, and incorporate the elements into a younger, more appropriate story aimed at an elementary school student.

"You want to write a story about an adulterer for seven year olds?" I take off my jacket, turn a chair around backwards to sit, and jump right into the middle of the debate.

"Not a story about an adulterer…we can make it about a less mature type of sin…but I think the main points, the moral of the story, can be simplified easily enough." Allie says.

"Zack, help me here. Tell these two that *Scarlet Letter* is a chick book and we should do something a little more interesting." Keller leans back in his chair, hands locked behind his head, waiting for me to defend his position.

I look over at Allie. Her eyes are gleaming. "I don't know, Keller, *Scarlet Letter* might work."

Allie smiles victoriously, giving Keller no time to rebut. "So it's settled, our book is Scarlet Letter…how about we each write down what lesson we think the book is supposed to teach and then swap papers and see if we can come up with a way to relate the message to young kids."

It takes a little convincing from the three of us, but Keller agrees to give Allie's idea a try. Nine o'clock rolls around too quickly and the librarian is practically kicking us out as we finally decide the plot for our storybook. I'm the only one with a car tonight, so I offer to drive everyone home. I drop off Cory and Keller first, even though they live closer to me and it would've made more sense to drop them off after Allie.

I pull up in front of Allie's house, our comfortable conversation falling into a lull. Suddenly there's uneasiness between us. At least that's what I feel, although I'm not sure Allie feels the same way. Or maybe she's just really good at hiding it. "So, are you going to the bonfire Saturday night?" I ask.

"I was thinking about it."

"You should go," I say, with a hint of desperation in my voice that surprises even me when I hear it.

Allie smiles, turning to face me. It's dark, but I can see the green in her eyes light up. "Okay. *Maybe* I will."

"Then *maybe* I'll see you there," I tease.

She giggles and leans forward and kisses me on the cheek. "Thanks for the ride home, Zack."

"No problem." I watch her walk to the door, telling myself it's the gentlemanly thing to do…make sure she gets in the house okay and all. But the way my eyes stay glued to her every step of the way is anything but gentlemanly.

Pulling into my driveway, I wait patiently as the garage door slowly rolls up. Across the street, the light is on in Emily's room. I'm sure she left it on to tell me she's awake. Her parents' car isn't in the driveway yet.

I get out of the car in the garage, and press the button to lower the door. There's time for me to duck underneath, but instead I watch the door creep down until it reaches the floor and Emily's house is no longer in sight. I'm sure I'll get an earful tomorrow morning for not coming by. But tonight, it just doesn't feel like the right thing to do.

Chapter 7

Nikki—

Brookside, Texas

When I look out the kitchen window for the twentieth time in the last hour, Ashley tries to get me to relax. "Never thought I'd see the day where you're anxious to see Evil Evans," she teases.

"What if she didn't find her?"

"She did. Don't worry."

Four long days of waiting, not hearing a word from Ms. Evans, had me convinced that I was just a file to her. Not a person whose future depended on her being able to spend more than an hour on one of the forty-plus kids in her caseload. Until today, when she called and said she needed to talk to me.

"You don't know that," I say.

"Yes. I do."

"No, you don't." My words come out a bit curt. It's a tone I've never taken with Ashley and her eyebrows arch in surprise.

"I may not have heard the words, but I know it in my heart. I know things have to work out for you, Nikki."

"What makes you so sure?" I murmur.

The sound of tires pulling into the trailer's gravel driveway saves Ashley from having to answer. She slips out with a weak smile. I have the door open waiting before Ms. Evans even exits her car.

"You look tired today, Nikki." She glances around at the sparse furnishings and sighs. "Why don't we sit down?"

My heart lurches in my chest. The doctors always asked me to sit whenever they had to deliver bad news. I wonder if adults think I might fall over if they tell me something I don't want to hear. Something irrational inside of me tells me that if I stand, she won't be able to give me bad news.

"I'd rather stand." I say, trying my best to not come off difficult. I'm in no mood to waste time debating the benefits of sitting versus standing.

Ms. Evans takes a deep breath and looks at me for a minute before nodding and sitting down herself. She takes out an oversized leather planner, the zipper bulging to contain all of the different manila folders shoved inside. Shuffling though at least a dozen worn folders with notes scribbled all over their outsides, she stops at one and pulls it out from the pile. It's fatter than all the others.

"I found your Aunt, Nikki."

Excited. Scared. Nervous. Anxious. I decide to sit after all.

"She wants to meet you."

"Really?" My heart races with excitement. "Where is she?"

"She's here, in Texas."

"She lives in Texas?" My hopes raised, there's no hiding how I feel. Ms. Evans reads my face and I see her expression falter.

"No. I'm afraid she lives in California"

"So why is she in Texas? Did she come to see me?"

"She came in for your mother's funeral."

My eyes widen. I've seen my Aunt and don't even know it. "Really?"

"Yes. She thinks she saw you in the parking lot when she pulled in. But you looked upset and she didn't want to make it worse by approaching you."

"But…but Mom's funeral was a week ago. Why is she still here?"

"She's been trying to figure out what to do. She wasn't sure if she should reach out to you."

"And now she wants to meet me? Why?"

"What do you mean, why? I thought you'd be thrilled with the news."

I am happy. At least I think I am…but something makes me feel even more unsettled than before Ms. Evans came in to tell me my fate. "She wants to see me to decide if she wants to take me, doesn't she?"

"It's not like that, Nikki."

"Has she agreed to take me?" I ask pointedly.

"No. But she hasn't said no either."

"So she's undecided."

"I think she wants to do what's best for you. She wants to meet you. Get to know you a little better."

Great. A test. Just what I need now. "When?"

"Tomorrow."

Pushing panic aside, I do my best not to show fear. "Okay."

Ms. Evans smiles at me. If I didn't know better, I'd almost think she likes me today.

"I'll pick you up at noon and you two can have lunch. Get to know each other a bit."

As if I had any other choice, I force a smile and nod.

I tear through all of my taped boxes and Ashley's entire closet, trying to decide what to wear. There's just no outfit that screams, *I'm a kid you never met, but you should let me live with you anyway.* I finally settle for jeans and a pink shirt. The shirt is a bit frou-frou for my taste, but Ashley swears it makes me look sweet and innocent. I'll take any help I can get.

The whole ride to the restaurant we're meeting my Aunt at, Ms. Evans tries to make small talk, but I'm too nervous to participate much. I stare out the window, watching the trailer parks fade into the distance as Houston gets closer and closer.

"Mrs. Nichols is very nice, I think you'll like her." Evil Evans says as we pull into a parking lot.

"Mrs. Nichols? Is that what I should call her? I guess she's married?" I'd gone over so many things in my head…thought I was thoroughly prepared for today, but already there's two things I haven't even thought of. What do I call her? And what if she's married and already has kids? Maybe they won't want another mouth to feed.

"Relax." Ms. Evans reaches down and covers my hand with hers. I'm not sure why, but I let her.

"I think you can call her Claire, or Mrs. Nichols if that makes you more comfortable. And, no, she isn't married. She's a widow."

"How did her husband die?" I have no idea why I ask the question, but I really want to know the answer for some reason.

"I didn't ask, Nikki."

"I guess I shouldn't either?" It's more of a question than a statement.

"I think you'll be fine. You ask what you need to ask. This needs to work for both of you. Not just Mrs. Nichols." She pats the hand she's still holding.

I take a deep breath and blow out an exaggerated exhale.

"Are you ready?"

"As I'll ever be."

Claire Nichols is nothing like I expected. She's tall, unlike the petite size my mother and I are. Or were. The petite size my mother was. Her hair is pulled back from her face in a simple ponytail, yet it leaves her looking sophisticated and stylish. She's wearing a sweater set and skirt, very modern and pretty.

Ms. Evans makes the awkward introductions and leaves us after only a few minutes to deal with another emergency. The second one that's come up during the two hours I've been with her.

"How are you holding up, Nikki?" It seems to be a popular question that grownups like to ask. Very generic, open ended.

"I'm fine."

"Really?" Claire waits till she catches my gaze. Her eyes take my breath away. They're the same as Mom's, pale blue with a dark ring of greenish blue around the outside.

"You have Mom's eyes." The words tumble from my lips and I hear them wobble as they reach the air.

Claire smiles hesitantly. "Our mom used to say if it wasn't for our eyes, she'd never believe we were sisters."

"You weren't a lot alike, I guess."

She shakes her head. "You have her eyes too."

"I know."

"Did you know your mom had a sister, Nikki?"

Unsure what the right answer is, I lie. "Yes." Claire taking me home with her is step one in my plan to find my own sister. I need to make her think my mom would have really wanted me to be with her. My guess is that's actually the furthest thing from the truth, since Mom didn't tell me she had a sister until *after* she died.

"I'm surprised," Claire says, and I can see the shock on her face. She isn't lying.

"My mother said she was sorry she stopped speaking to you a long time ago. She regretted it, Aunt Claire." I force the *Aunt* in, hoping it might help. Shoot…she looks skeptical.

"She did? I mean, no disrespect to your mom. She was my sister, after all, but in all the years I spent with her, I never saw her show any regret. I thought it was something that her…" She stops abruptly, looking as if she's said something wrong. Is she afraid to mention Mom's illness, or does she think I don't know Mom was mentally ill? I lived with her for seventeen years. How could she think I didn't know?

"I know all about my mom's illness. She needed me to know so I could help her. Plus, it wasn't exactly an easy thing to hide, if you know what I mean."

A combination of relief and dread wash over her pale pretty face. It's something I'm used to. Nobody wants to talk to a kid about mental illness. People would feel more comfortable telling a child her mother has cancer than that she has a psychiatric disease. Mental illness is taboo in society. I don't get it. I never have. But I've learned to deal with it. Everyone was so comfortable talking about Mom's diabetes— a condition she was born with and one she needed to take insulin for her entire life. But when the conversation turned to the illness in Mom's head, everyone got afraid.

"It's a difficult subject to talk about, isn't it?" Claire's thoughts seem far away. "She was my sister and I still have a tough time with it. I guess it's because, as kids, our mom never talked about it. All the focus was on your mother's diabetes and her medications for that. Everything else was treated as a secret until we were teenagers. And by then, the things my parents didn't speak of, the things I didn't understand, had driven a real wedge between your mom and me."

Intimate conversations like this with a stranger make me nervous. I try to hide it, but Claire sees right through it, "We don't need to talk about this now. It's too much too fast. I'm sorry."

I always get a cold feeling in my body when I feel like someone knows what I'm thinking. I rub my hands together to try and make it disappear.

"I live in California, Nikki. Do you know that? It's where your mother and I were born and raised."

We've moved a dozen times, but never outside of Texas. I just assumed Mom was from here. I didn't know she was raised in California but I'm not sure I should admit it. "Do you have children?" I ask instead.

Claire's face turns sad. "No, I don't. It wasn't meant to be for me. I lost my husband before we ever had any."

"How much older than Mom are you?" I ask, immediately hoping that I didn't just stick my foot in my mouth. Why do I assume she's the older sister?

"Three years. I was three when your mom was born. Just turned twenty-five when you were born."

I always knew Mom was young when I was born, but it's weird to think she was only a few years older than I am now when she gave birth to me...and to my sister. I can't even imagine having one baby, let alone two, now, and with all of her medical problems.

Mom's age is really the only detail I've ever known about my birth. And that her diabetes got much worse after the pregnancy— another pregnancy would probably have ended her life. I remember a doctor telling her that when I was seven or eight. I don't know why, but the conversation stuck with me all these years.

After that, Mom had to have an insulin pump placed in her body. It sat on the outside of her waist in a little pouch; insulin was sent through a plastic tube into her body to help her pancreas work. Mom treated so many things in our life like a paranoid secret, that I've always hung on tightly to the facts.

Claire eases the conversation into less intrusive topics— school, travel, hobbies. We even find we have a few things in common: we both like to read, neither of us can swim and math isn't our strongpoint.

Ms. Evans checks in with us a few times, but doesn't stick around to talk. Eventually, there's a lull in our conversation. After a long, deafening moment of silence, Claire locks eyes with me and softly asks, "What do you want to happen here, Nikki?"

The point-blank question catches me off guard, freezing me. I can't just blurt out, "I want to find my sister." Claire hasn't mentioned her, and Mom warned in her letter that Claire wouldn't help me find her and probably wouldn't even admit I was a twin.

"I don't know what I want, Aunt Claire." I pause, choosing my words carefully. "I want my mom back, but I know that isn't something anyone can give me. I don't want to go to a foster home. That's what I know I don't want."

"I'd like to help you, Nikki. You're my niece. I want what's best for you but I don't know if I'm it. I don't want to be selfish. Maybe we can go day by day and see what each day brings? Do you think you could leave your friends and your life in Texas and start over in California? It's a lot to think about, isn't it?"

There's nothing I need to think about. My mind is already made up. But if she thinks it's a big decision, I'll pretend I have to think about it. Although nothing could stop me from going.

After lunch, Aunt Claire talks to Ms. Evans. They decide it would be best to try to arrange for me to stay a few months with Ashley's family so I can finish school here. It's already March and Aunt Claire can't enroll me in school in California until a judge grants her temporary custody, which might take a while.

Later, Ashley's mom agrees to let me live with them while Aunt Claire goes back to California to work. Of course, the state of

Texas paying Ashley's mom money to keep me has more to do with her decision than my actual wellbeing.

I'm surprised when Aunt Claire says she's going to come back and forth every ten days to spend time with me until the hearing is scheduled. I just keep hoping it isn't a continued test that I might eventually fail.

Chapter 8

Zack—

Long Beach, California

"You're not going to wear that, are you?" Emily barks from the bottom of my driveway.

"It's too early to fight, Em. It's Saturday. I can wear whatever I want. I'm washing the car," I respond, not even looking up from the bucket of water I'm filling.

"*Zack!*" Emily bellows as she walks up the driveway.

Stopping what I'm doing, I look up, seeing a face full of frustration. I also now see she's dressed in a new white dress. One that makes me glad that I have a hose of cold water nearby. The tight little dress hugs her sexy curves, and dozens of silver bracelets shine atop her perfectly tanned skin. I follow the hem of her short skirt down her toned, mile-high legs until I reach her strappy silver sandals.

"I mean tonight. You're not going to wear that tonight! Are you?"

"It's ten in the morning, Em. I haven't thought about tonight or my wardrobe."

"Zack!" she scolds, as she moves into my personal space, intentionally brushing up against me.

It's been three days of holy hell because I didn't race up to her room after the library the other night. I didn't even know if she still intended to go to the bonfire down at the beach tonight. But I guess I should have known. Emily never misses a social event, especially the one celebrating the end of our junior year. She never wants to be seen without being on my arm, always needing me to play Ken to her Barbie.

"You still want to go to the bonfire?" I ask.

"Of course I want to go! Everyone expects us to be there." Moving in closer so I can feel her breath on my neck, Emily says in a low, sexy voice, "Do you like my dress? I bought it just for you. For *after* the bonfire. You still want tonight to be our first time, don't you?"

"I can't wait, Em," I say, hoping I sound more enthused than I feel.

"Careful with my dress. You want me to wear it later and look perfect. Don't you?"

Do I want her in the dress? Is that a trick question? I go with the right answer instead of what I really want to say. "Yes, of course, Em. You look gorgeous. You'll be the most beautiful girl at the bonfire. But you look great in anything. So why don't you go change and wash the car with me?"

A couple of years ago Emily would have ran upstairs and changed her clothes. But so many things have changed. Emily's changed. I've changed.

"Be ready at six," she yells, ignoring my offer. "This is going to be the best night of our lives, Zack. I promise."

44

When Emily slips into the passenger seat of my car at just after six, my body reacts on its own. She looks beyond incredible tonight.

"Well, how do I look?" Obviously Emily knows the answer. She has four mirrors in her bedroom for god's sake. And she spends all of her spare time looking in them.

"Gorgeous. You've never looked more beautiful, Em." I'm not lying a bit. Her smooth, tanned skin glows against the tight white dress. Her long, thick, wavy blonde hair lies flawlessly around her high, firm breasts. She'll catch the eye of every guy tonight…which is exactly what she wants. Who needs the damned bonfire? "Let's stay home and just hang out me and you, Em. I don't want to share you with anyone tonight? What if we ride our bikes down on the boardwalk like we used to?"

Apparently *that* was the wrong thing to say. "Go bike riding? Really Zack?" Emily screeches. "This is the biggest night of the year! We *have* to go."

"Alright, Em," I say sounding like a good little boy as I start to back out of the driveway. She doesn't even notice I'm deflated.

Emily chatters the whole way there about who is going to be there, who is dating who, and other superficial nonsense that I can't, nor want to, keep track of.

As we exit the car in the beach parking lot, the bonfire party can already be heard roaring off in the near distance. Dozens of cars arrive just as we do and it only takes a minute before Emily and I are surrounded by people.

"Oh my god, you look so stunning," one of Emily's devout harem members squeals. It's the first of many squeals, as Emily and I are quickly pulled apart so that the girls can surround her and pay her compliments. I try not to roll my eyes.

A familiar voice catches my attention. "You look lost." I turn to find Allie smiling at me. She'd been grabbing something from her trunk and I almost walked past without noticing her.

Allie's smile is contagious. It's sincere, not for show. No court of friends surrounding her. Wearing shorts and a t-shirt, she holds a volleyball in her hands. A ponytail loosely ties back her long, dark hair. *She* certainly hasn't been getting ready since ten this morning. But somehow I think I like her look better. Emily would freak if she knew that…but it's the truth. Sure, Emily looks gorgeous tonight, but her beauty is one-dimensional, the kind I'm realizing fades quickly.

"Planning on taking me on?" I tease in a way that, in all honesty, borders on flirting. My eyes point to the volleyball and then meet her gaze with a smirk.

Her face flushes, but she gives it right back to me. "Think you can take me, Zack? I might surprise you."

Whoa…I better walk away now. Emily would spot what was going on in a heartbeat. Her other-woman meter is the most sensitive organ in her body.

Just as Allie and I hit the sand and start to join the large crowd, I see Emily laughing and posing in the center of a group of wanna-be-Emily girls. I look from Emily to Allie and go with my brain instead of my gut.

"I hope I see you later, Allie," I say, meaning it, as I walk off to join Emily. For a night that is supposed to be a night all about me and Emily, it sure isn't starting off that way.

"Zack, where did you go?" Emily demands. With the crowd surrounding her, she might as well be on stage. A stage where she comes alive, performing.

"I lost you in the crowd for a minute. I'm right here. Relax."

Grabbing my hand, she pulls me into the inner circle. "Stay with us. The fun is all here."

The "fun" consists of taking Instagram pictures of me and Em in front of the bonfire, Em listening intently to every piece of gossip her friends share, and me standing within an inch of her side at all times.

Dylan, the boyfriend of one of the girls Emily is currently gossiping with, looks as glazed over as I do. He's a college freshman and, no doubt, tired of this scene by now too. We exchange glances and Dylan shakes his head. A minute later he tells his girlfriend he's going to play in a nearby volleyball game. He asks me to join him. It's a perfect excuse to escape the torture I've been enduring since we got here. Surprisingly, Emily smiles when I tell her I'm going with Dylan. I'm sure she thinks it's cool I'm going to hang out with a college freshman.

After tearing off his t-shirt, to the pleasure of the junior class, Dylan smiles. "Let's go have fun and let them stand around and play with their phones." Thank god there's one sensible person in this crowd.

Dylan is the star of the game within minutes of entering it. I'm not playing half bad myself. The volleyball crowd is definitely different than Em's crowd. There's trash talking, diving for the ball, and people don't care if they are sweaty messes. Finally, some fun.

Halfway through the game, several players on the other side get yanked away to other things and they sub in a few new opponents. I look up and find Allie directly across the net from me. I grin and yell over, "Oh, so you're gonna take me on after all, are you?"

Allie beams back a smile and serves the ball right at me. It should have been an easy volley, but I miss because I can't seem to peel my eyes away from her smile. She just looks so happy and carefree. My missing evens up the score and elicits some spirited teasing and laughter from those around us— enough uproar to catch

47

Emily's attention, I guess. I don't realize it at first, but she's standing courtside, seething.

"I was distracted. You got lucky on that one," I tease as Allie serves her next shot. The ball travels back and forth a few times and then I rush the net and spike it down on the other side. Dylan and I high-five and it's my turn to serve. "This one's just for you, Allie." I toss the ball high in the air and wail it across the net as hard as I can, still smiling. They miss. Allie sticks her tongue out at me— and that's when I finally spot Emily on the sidelines.

She lets the anger burn in her gaze just long enough to catch everyone's attention, then she turns and storms off, her crowd of minions following her.

"Just let her cool off. She'll get over it." Dylan says, shrugging his shoulders and shaking his head. Feeling like I haven't done anything wrong, I'm not even sure if I care if he's right. I let her go.

Half an hour later, I find Emily sitting around the bonfire in the middle of her crowd. "Wanna go for a walk?" I ask quietly, offering my hand to help her up. I swear I hear the buzz start before we even walk away. It's either gossip or be gossiped about with this crew.

"Listen, Em," I say when we're out of earshot of the crowd. "I was playing a game. You know how competitive I get. Hell, you're the same way. I don't know why you got so upset."

Emily stops and turns to face me. "You really don't know why I'm so upset?"

"I'm guessing it's because I was teasing Allison, but I don't know why that would upset you. She's just a friend."

"Why is she a friend? That's the part I don't get, Zack. We have so many friends, why do you need to hang out with people like her?"

"Wait. So you're not *jealous* of Allison?"

48

"*Jealous?* Why would I be jealous of *her?*" She practically laughs at the notion.

"Let me get this straight. You're mad because I was having fun with people you don't consider cool enough to hang out with?" Disgust laces my voice, but she either doesn't notice or doesn't care.

"Yes, Zack. You're ruining everything."

"Ruining everything? What are you talking about?"

"Everything is so perfect right now." She folds her arms across her chest, reminding me of a spoiled child about to throw a tantrum. "We have the best friends, they're just like us, I don't get why that's not enough for you."

"Are you listening to yourself?" If I wasn't so shocked, I'd probably be angrier. "Emily, you don't pick friends by their social status or what they look like. I want friends that have fun, not pose and sit around caring about what other people think of them."

"And you don't have fun with us?" The pitch of her voice rises a few octaves.

"No. Actually, I don't." I feel a sense of relief admitting it. Saying it out loud makes me feel true to myself. Finally.

Emily's expression is scathing. "You are so not getting what you think you're getting when we get home."

And there it is, the chip she keeps anteing up. She's staring up at me, waiting for me to grovel or try to fix what she thinks I've done wrong. Only, I don't want what she's dangling at the moment. Never thought I'd see the day when I wouldn't want inside of Emily Bennett. But right now, it's the furthest thing from my mind. Looking her straight in the eyes, I give her the god's honest truth. "You know what, Em. I'm not in the mood anyway."

Her jaw drops, the look of shock on her face is priceless. I'd really love to end this conversation by just walking away, but we've strayed pretty far from the crowd and I won't leave her to walk back alone.

"Come on. I'll walk you back to your friends."

"You'll be sorry tomorrow, Zack Martin. And, you know what, by then it may be too late." Nose high in the air, Emily struts back to the bonfire to rejoin the crowd.

At midnight, I try to get Emily to let me drive her home. Speaking or not, I brought her here and I feel responsible for taking her home. "Em," I say in a low voice, but loud enough so she can hear me.

Every single mouth in her gaggle of girls shushes and turns to face me. They anxiously wait on our exchange. Emily looks up at me, but says nothing.

"You want to get going?"

"I'm staying. I'll get a ride," she says the words expecting a reaction from me. Thinks I'll be upset that we aren't going home together, for things to happen as originally planned.

"Okay. Who's driving you?" It's an innocent question, one meant to make sure she gets home safely, although that's not how Emily chooses to hear it.

"Dylan will drive me." She smirks and I see her girlfriends trying to suppress smiles. I'm sure they all knew what was supposed to happen tonight and are proud of Emily for what they perceive is my punishment. "You shouldn't wait up."

"Okay, Emily. Get home safe."

Chapter 9

Zack—

Long Beach, California

I wake to the creak of my door and the sound of my mother calling my name. Pulling the covers up over my head, I try to drown out the sound. But something about her voice shakes me to my core. There's a thick tremble as she speaks. "Zack. Wake up." She sniffles.

My brain goes from groggy to high alert. My body bolts upright. She's crying. My mother does not cry. "What's wrong, Mom?" Assuming the worst, panic sets in. Something's happened to my father, I fear.

Her cries turn into sobs. She doesn't respond.

"Mom. Where's Dad?" My voice is growing louder.

More sobs. She slumps into me as her cry intensifies. Wrapping my arms around her back, I hold her, but my voice becomes more insistent. "Mom, what's going on? Where's Dad?" My own tears start to well, even though I'm still in the dark over what we're crying about.

"He's downstairs," she finally spits out, breathless between sobs.

"What happened, Mom?"

"It's Emily."

My heart clenches in my chest.

"What?" My voice rises to a yell. "Mom, what about Emily?"

She cries more. My father comes to the door. I turn, catching sight of him. He's been crying too. My heart jumps into my throat.

"Zack." My father takes a deep breath. "Emily's been in an accident, son."

Nausea overwhelms me, my head spins, but I force myself from the bed. "Where is she?" I'm yanking on clothes as I speak.

"Long Beach University Hospital."

Frantically, I search my desk for my keys, then take off down the stairs. My father shouts for me to wait, but I'm out the door before he can catch up to me. He rips open the passenger door just as I'm backing out and jumps in.

Pacing the ER waiting area like a caged lion, I wait and wait for what seems like forever. My mother arrives carrying my shoes. Looking down, I'm surprised to find I don't have any on.

"Did you hear anything yet?" She whispers to my father.

He shakes his head and wraps his arm around her shoulder, pulling her to him tightly.

Finally, after what seems like days, Emily's parents emerge from the double doors that block her from me. I rush to them. Mr. Bennett looks at me and shakes his head no. *No? What does he mean, no?* My father comes to stand next to me. Mrs. Bennett finally looks up and, seeing me, she completely breaks down. Wailing, she falls to the floor.

My breathing comes faster and shorter. *I feel dizzy.* My thoughts spin so fast I can't see. They only stop when my entire world goes dark.

Chapter 10

Zack—

Long Beach, California - 2 days later

I stand in the parking lot alone, rain pelts down on me so hard it should sting, but I feel no pain. I feel nothing. Hollow. A shell of a body incapable of emotion. I look down at my navy suit, the one I wore to the homecoming dance with Emily, it's soaked through, clinging tightly against my body. Squeezing my eyes shut, I pray to a god I'm not sure I believe in anymore, begging him to take the image that was just seared into my brain from my memory. But it's no use, closing my eyes only makes the visual of her lying there even more vivid. I force them back open to chase what I see away, but it doesn't work. Visions of Emily lying there, so still, so peaceful, consume me. Her normally glowing, tanned skin is pale and dull, gray replacing the bronze and pink sun drenched color.

My body begins to shake, sobs racking through me even before my tears begin to fall. It's the first time I've cried since it happened. Time goes by, but I have no idea how long I stand there letting days of pent-up emotions wash over me. Eventually, the heavy rain begins to dwindle, my tears following its lead.

"Zack?" My father's voice is low, cautious. It's the same timid way everyone has spoken to me the last two days. I don't respond. I've barely said two words to anyone since it happened. "Come back inside, son. The minister is going to start soon."

My mother waits just inside the door, the same look of worry plastered across her face that she's worn since she woke me that morning. The morning everything changed. She puts her arm around me and together we walk slowly toward the room. The smell of flowers wafts in the air as we step closer, making me nauseous.

Jefferson Funeral Parlor is large; three separate viewing rooms normally hold multiple services. But today it's all for Emily. The retractable doors between rooms are open so that there's room for hundreds to sit. It's still not enough. People line the room, wall to wall. Family, friends, teachers, strangers. The line to visit the casket leads out the front door and halfway around the block. Everyone is here except for the driver who is still fighting for his own life at Long Beach University Hospital. The front of the car took the brunt of the impact when Dylan swerved to avoid a truck that veered into oncoming traffic. Amazingly, the rest of the passengers walked away with only minor cuts and bruises.

A quiet hush comes over the room as we walk in. Heads turn in our direction. The minister takes his position at the front of the room, silencing the murmur without words. Slowly, my parents lead me to the front row. I feel all the eyes in the room watching me, even though I don't look up.

Three chairs wait for our return. Mr. Bennett insisted we sit with him. I was Emily's family as much as he was, he said. I thought the weight of my guilt might be enough to pull me through the floor.

Ahead of us, a small table sits on one side of the ornate wooden casket, a tribute to Emily's life. A shrine. Four pictures in frames highlighting the life of the girl I loved: Her parents with her at her communion. Her junior yearbook picture. Me and Emily all dressed up for junior prom. But it's the last one that gets to me, rips a hole right through my already torn heart. Emily riding her canary yellow Schwinn. Memories flood back to me…the day I met her, the first time she let me ride it. Her on the handlebars chattering away as I peddled us to the park where we'd play on the swings for hours. It breaks me. Tears roll down my face uncontrollably, my shoulders shuddering, each breath between sobs burning my throat.

The minister begins to speak. Words flow from his mouth, yet I don't hear anything he says. To my left, my dad hangs tough, tightening his grip around my shoulder. To my right, my mother silently sobs alone. I can't even bring myself to comfort her. Long minutes go by, the haze I'm in blocking me from reality until a verse catches my attention.

"We cannot judge a biography by its length.
Nor by the number of pages in it.
We must judge it by the richness of its contents.
Sometimes those unfinished are among the most poignant.
We can not judge a song by its duration.
Nor by the number of its notes.
We must judge it by the way it touches and lifts our souls.
Sometimes those unfinished are among the most beautiful.
And when something has enriched your life.
And when its melody lingers on in your heart.
Is it unfinished?
Or is it endless?"

Graveside, hours later, I stand watching an endless stream of mourners place a rose on Emily's casket before they walk away. Tears gone, I'm numb, inside and out. I watch, but don't really see. Touch, but don't really feel.

Eventually, only my family and Emily's parents remain surrounding the hole in the ground, where Emily's casket rests next to a mound of dirt. My father nudges me, speaking quietly, "Come on, Son. You need to say your goodbye and leave Emily's parents to do the same."

Mr. Bennett looks to me and then to Mrs. Bennett. Mrs. Bennett nods, a single tear falling from her eyes. "No, please, I think we should go. Emily would want Zack to be the last one here. She may have been my daughter, but her heart belonged to your son."

Placing his hand on my shoulder and squeezing as he walks by, Mr. Bennett's voice is choked up as he says quietly, "Say your goodbyes, son."

My parents walk to the waiting cars along with Emily's. Finally alone, I stand staring down at the pile of roses atop of the casket. Emily's final words to me come flooding back, the first memory I've allowed myself since it all happened. *"You'll be sorry tomorrow, Zack Martin. And, you know what, by then it may be too late."*

Falling to my knees in the muddy grass, I cry. And I cry and I cry. Until there's no more tears left to come.

Chapter 11

Nikki—

Brookside, Texas - 5 months later

"This isn't permanent, Ash," I whisper so Aunt Claire and Ms. Evans can't hear. "I'll be back after I find her. I promise."

I mean it as I say it, but as soon as the words come out I start to wonder if I will really be back.

This morning, I stood in a courtroom while a judge granted my aunt temporary custody. I can't believe how fast time has gone by. The pain of losing Mom is still fresh, yet at the same time it feels like forever since I heard her voice. The mixed emotions on Ashley's face could be a mirror image of mine.

"I'm happy for you, Nikki," she says with a hesitant smile— the kind of smile you form when you don't know if you're happy or scared. I know she's scared— for both of us.

"Thank you for everything," I say, hugging Ashley tightly. I'm not normally a touchy-feely person, so this unexpected demonstration of affection makes Ash start to cry.

"Nikki, we have a lot to do before you can get on a flight with your Aunt tomorrow." Isn't that just like Evil Evans, not being sensitive enough to spot a moment between Ashley and me?

Aunt Claire steps in. "Why don't you come to the airport with us tomorrow, Ashley? We can have lunch and you can spend a little time together before our flight. The car service can take you back home after."

I feel like I'm Annie and I've just been adopted by Daddy Warbucks. Ashley squeals a thank you at Aunt Claire and squeezes me once again. At least I'll be departing Brookside in style.

As I pack up the last of my things in Ashley's trailer, I start to wonder if I've made the right decision. The way Aunt Claire looked at Donna and the dim, cramped trailer makes me wonder if she's looking at me the same way now. Whenever she's come to visit, Ms. Evans has always driven me to a restaurant or her hotel. Aunt Claire comes from a world where trailer parks don't exist. I don't know if that's the right world for me. This is the only life I've ever known.

I tuck away my thoughts, reminding myself that finding my sister is more important than my feeling a little uncomfortable. I don't intend to live with Aunt Claire forever, or even to stay in California. I just need to find my sister and figure out what to do from there.

"Almost ready, Nikki?" Aunt Claire asks as she comes in from bringing the next-to-last box from the trailer out to the waiting town car. "We have to get the boxes over to a delivery store. You know you have to pay just to take a bag on the plane these days. So, we'll ship whatever we can."

The truth is, I didn't know. I've never even been on a plane before. But I agree, pretending what she says makes sense.

Picking up the box I've purposely left for last, I ask, "Can I carry this small one on the plane with me? Will it count as a bag?"

Aunt Claire stares at the small cardboard box clutched in my hands. "Of course, you can carry anything that's important to you." Her voice gentle, she asks, "Is that box important? We could get a new box. That one looks just about ready to fall apart, I think. They sell them in the UPS package store we're going to."

"Just some of my mom's things and a few pictures. Things I've moved in the same box every time we moved." My own voice drops, becoming shaky, as I answer. It isn't easy to leave. Mom and I didn't live here that many years, but this is the first time I've ever moved *without* her.

Aunt Claire's face turns solemn. I'm not sure if it's because I mentioned Mom or because I mentioned moving around a lot. I get the feeling Aunt Claire feels badly that I've had what she thinks must have been a crappy life, full of moving over and over again.

"I'm sorry, Nikki. I can't image how hard this is for you. You must miss your mother. I'm so sorry, honey." Tears gently roll down her face. I've never seen anyone cry in such a polite, pretty way before.

"She was also your sister." I don't look at her as I say the next words. "I'd imagine that it's just as hard to lose a sister. At least I got to spend most of my time with her...you weren't that lucky."

Aunt Claire nods solemnly. I turn to look for Ash, so we can leave, but she's nowhere in sight. Instead, Donna has snuck up behind me.

"We're going to miss you, honey," she says, holding out her arms. If Aunt Claire is Daddy Warbucks, Donna is playing the part of Miss Hannigan to a tee. She hasn't called me honey in the five hundred times I've walked through her door. I'm suddenly conscious of the smell of her cigarettes and cheap perfume.

Left Behind

At the door, I turn back to take one last look around, sending a silent prayer to Mom: I promise I won't let California change me, no matter what.

Chapter 12

Zack—

Long Beach, California

I hear the door bell ring but I don't leave my room. That's the way it's been every day since it happened. People came by a lot more in the beginning. Friends from school, neighbors, my aunt and cousins. It took five months, but the stream of well-wishers has finally slowed down. Maybe that's the way it happens. Time just has a way of making things ease up. For me? Nothing has dulled the pain since Emily died.

My mom's talking to someone downstairs but I don't recognize the voice. That's happened a lot too lately. I hear things, but nothing registers. Voices and words all jumble together and it all sounds the same. Nothing sparks my interest, nothing brings me out of my haze.

The talking stops again. I guess whoever came by has left. People don't stick around long since Emily died. Even my parents, who come in my room a dozen times a day, maybe more, leave quickly.

There's a knock at my bedroom door but I don't bother to get up. Mom and Dad don't wait for me to answer anyway. They knock once and come in. I get the feeling they're afraid of what they might find if they wait to knock a second time.

A second knock. That breaks my trance and I look to the door. A third knock is accompanied by a low voice, "Zack, your mom told me it was okay to come up. Can I come in?" She pauses and then softly adds, "Please."

Even through the dull fog I recognize Allie's voice. Or am I imagining it? Is she really on the other side of my bedroom door? I say nothing and the voice goes silent. Maybe I was wrong. Maybe there is no voice.

The door opens with a creak. I don't know whether to yell and tell her to leave, or just go back to staring at the ceiling from my bed. I decide ignoring her is the less painful option. Maybe she'll just go away.

From the corner of my eye I see her pull my desk chair close to my bed and sit down. I close my eyes.

"Zack, I know you don't want to see anyone. I tried emails and texts and phone calls. I just thought maybe if I came here…" She trails off. There's a tremble in her voice when she continues. "Maybe there's something I can do. I want to help you."

Allie's voice is warm and tender and it pulls my eyes away from the ceiling. I roll into a sitting position so I feel less vulnerable. Just as my eyes make contact with hers, a tear rolls from her left eye. Even in the darkness of my unlit room I can see she's crying. People shouldn't cry over me. I don't deserve it.

Instinctively, I reach out to wipe the tear. Before I reach Allie's face the rest of my mind snaps awake and I pull my hand back quickly. Allie reaches out for my hand. It's the first thing I feel in months. Her skin, soft and gentle, only a whisper of a touch, yet it's so strong and overwhelming. The contact starts to pull me into the present world. But I don't want to be there. I don't want to be anywhere without Emily. I pull my hand away as though I've been scorched.

Unfazed, Allie tries again. "Zack, you don't have to say anything. I know I can't fix anything. I just wanted to see you. Even if we don't talk."

Something inside compels me. "Thank you. I read your emails and your texts," I lie. I haven't opened anything anyone's sent. "Thank you for thinking of me."

Even in the unlit room I can see the glimmer of hope in her eyes when I respond. Is that how my parents feel? Are they just waiting for me to speak?

Allie smiles, but this smile doesn't reach her eyes...not even close. It's sad and forced. Something makes me smile back. I don't want her to look so sad. Her smile responds to mine, growing real, not forced. I remember how I always liked that smile. It was almost too big— almost, but not quite.

"Aren't you dying to know how *The Scarlet Letter* turned out in English? I figured the anticipation would be gut wrenching. It's the real reason why I had to come," Allie teases, her words coming quickly, hoping to keep me in the here and now. I never went back to school after the accident. Our English project wasn't even a thought all these months.

"Yes, Allie. I was worried. Very worried that some second grader hasn't been able to read about hookers wearing the letter "A" on their boobs." The sarcasm feels good. Normal.

She giggles. "Mr. Hartley saved our story to read to the class last. I think he was scared, Zack."

Her laugh is contagious. I don't have to think about it, it just comes naturally. But then I catch myself. I don't deserve to laugh. It's not fair to Emily. I slam the shutter back down over the window of happiness she's opened.

"Listen, Allie...thanks for stopping by. It was nice of you, but I'm really tired and need to catch some sleep." I stand, leaving no room for interpretation that it's time for her to go.

Allie's smile falters. She stands. "I'm not going to let you get off that easy, Zack. I'm coming back to read you our story soon." She tries to sound enthusiastic.

She tucks the chair neatly back under my desk, then turns to me, a nervous smile on her face. Reaching up on her toes, she kisses me innocently on the cheek. "If there is anything I can do, I'd like to be here for you, Zack."

Emily doesn't deserve the disrespect we're showing her. "She died because she was jealous of me being with you that night, Allie. Please go."

Like a coward, I fixate my eyes on the floor so I don't have to see her face, not looking up until I hear the door close.

It's August and the weather is intensely warm. Waiting until after my parents leave to run some Saturday morning errands, I throw on my running gear and head outside. While I stretch, my eyes can't help but wander across the street. My chest tightens just seeing Emily's house, knowing she'll never walk in the door again. Knowing her parents want nothing more than for the past five months all to have been a nightmare. How the hell am I supposed to stay here? Walk in and out of my house every day, a constant reminder of what we've lost? What I've done.

Without finishing my stretches, I take off. No warm up. No slow start. Just full out running. Running away as fast as I can, praying the distance eases the pain. The thick humid air makes breathing difficult, each desperate inhale burns my lungs, but it's not enough. I need more. More pain, more distance, more suffering.

64

Four miles fly by in record time, my body giving out on me, unable to endure the strain my mind demands of it. Doubled over, panting heavily, my hands on my knees, I struggle to catch my breath. I'm not even sure where I am. Although I really don't give a shit. I have nowhere I need to be and no one who needs me. Anymore.

Hours pass and I alternate between running and walking. Before I know it, the sun is setting and I find myself in front of the cemetery. Emily's cemetery. I make my way through the large iron gates, looking around at the endless rows of headstones, wondering if I can even find my way back to her gravesite. The place is huge, there must be twenty thousand stones and miles upon miles of roads and walkways that all look the same to me.

So I start walking. I know Emily probably won't have a stone yet, but her grandfather does. He's buried right next to her. A few people linger, passing by as I walk slowly, reading row after row of names. Each time I put my head down to avoid eye contact whenever someone nears.

Hours after darkness falls, I finally find her again. The ground is still raw with new dark dirt…fresh, just like the memory of losing her. I sit, leaning my back up against her grandfather's stone, and the tears start to fall. And fall and fall, until I'm sobbing so hard, it's hard to catch my breath. Eventually, exhausted and cried empty, I fall asleep, lying splayed across Emily's grave.

A hand on my shoulder startles me awake. I crack one eye open and glance up at my father as he sits down next to me. "Your mother's been worried sick," he says, gently rather than scolding. "I know it's hard, but you're going to have to let some of it out sooner or later, son. You can't keep it all to yourself." He wraps his arm around my shoulder. "We're worried about you. I know you need some space…and I'm going to try to give that to you. But don't scare us like you did today, disappearing for so long." My father quiets for a moment and then calls my name, gently, but firm in that fatherly way, "Zack." He forces me to look up, waits until I look right into his eyes. "Okay?"

"Okay."

Chapter 13

Nikki—

Long Beach, California

The house is nothing like I expected. Vibrant framed pictures decorate the warm colored walls, making it feel more like a home than anyplace I've ever lived. Yet sleep didn't come easy last night. The first night in a new place never does. I should know, I've had plenty of first nights.

Forcing myself from bed earlier than I need to, I take the time to explore with Aunt Claire gone to run errands for a few hours. My first stop— the framed photos on the mantel above the fireplace. Not wanting to appear too nosey, I've glanced but haven't had a chance to really take a good look.

The first photo is of two little girls, their arms wrapped around each other's shoulder while they smile brightly for the camera. The taller girl is holding a garden hose and has a mischievous grin on her face; the younger girl is drenched from head to toe. I almost don't recognize Mom with that easy, carefree smile.

It makes me wonder if she was born broken or if something happened after that photo to make her the way she was by the time I was born.

The photo next to it was taken at Aunt Claire's graduation from nursing school. She looks the same, only younger. The older woman beside her, my grandmother, a woman I've never seen, smiles proudly at her daughter dressed in an all-white uniform.

I pick up the largest of the photos, running my finger along the outline of the etched glass frame, studying the picture of the happy couple on their wedding day. Aunt Claire looks beautiful in a traditional white wedding dress, the kind you see on television with a long train and a veil that covers her face. Her husband is dressed in a simple dark suit; a huge smile lights up his face as he looks down at his new bride. They both look so happy, I get an ache in my chest thinking of how she must have felt when she lost him.

I turn, contemplating what I feel as I take in the entirety of the room…the pictures, the furniture, the bookshelves filled with books…it's all just so…normal. A feeling I'm entirely not used to.

My face is buried in a book when Aunt Claire comes in carrying groceries a few hours later.

"How did you sleep?" she asks, as I follow her out to the car to help her get the rest of the bags.

I shrug. "Okay, I guess." Why worry her that I tossed and turned half the night.

Aunt Claire smiles cautiously. "It will get easier. I promise. I always have trouble sleeping in a new place." Together, we begin to unpack the groceries. "I was thinking…how about we go get a new outfit for your first day of school Monday?"

I look down. "What's wrong with my clothes?" My voice comes out a bit defensively.

"Nothing. Nothing at all. It's just…my mother always bought us a new outfit for the first day of school. It was sort of a tradition." She smiles. "I always looked forward to it." Her smile falters a bit, her voice dipping lower and softer. "So did your mom. I thought maybe you would too." I find myself wondering what it would be like to go shopping with *my* sister. I really want to ask more questions, but it's too soon to risk poking around and making Aunt Claire suspicious of my intentions.

I agree to go shopping, although I'm not really sure I'll be sticking around long enough to create any traditions here.

By the end of the day, the new school outfit had exploded into three outfits, new exercise clothes, earbuds, a backpack and school supplies. At times, I actually had fun shopping with Aunt Claire.

Saturday morning, sporting new shorts, a tank top, and purple earbuds in my ears, I stand outside the front door and stretch my calves. I haven't exercised in almost a month, and the burn as I pull my foot back behind me to stretch my hamstring is a pain I welcome.

"Are you sure you remember the directions I gave you?" Aunt Claire comes outside and asks for the third time. She's worried I'll get lost on my run.

Smiling at her nervousness, I pull one ear bud from my ear. "Straight four blocks to Main, left two blocks to Arnold Ave, right on Front Street…that takes me to the high school track."

She looks relieved, a little bit at least. "You have your phone?"
I nod.

"Watch out for cars. Run with only one ear bud in so you can hear things around you."

"Always do. I'll be fine." I start off on my run, yelling back over my shoulder with a smile, "Give me an hour before you send out the helicopter search party, okay?"

I've never been a sports kid. Running is the only physical activity that I've ever participated in. Ashley liked to tease me that I was into running because it's one of the few sports where you don't have to be on a team. She wasn't entirely wrong. Running makes me feel in control, yet free at the same time. It clears my head, makes everything seem less complicated. Simpler.

Entering the track, I'm surprised to find it almost empty. Saturday morning is usually prime time for the jocks to get in their run. Then again, the grey clouds that were starting to roll in when I left the house twenty minutes ago are only starting to clear.

I take the first lap at a steady pace, preferring to alternate between sprinting and jogging, rather than the monotony of staying even paced for five full miles. A boy about my age is a half lap ahead of me the entire time I make my way around the cushioned track. Arriving at the point I started at again, I change gears, shifting from jogging to sprinting, quickly catching up— and passing— him.

Lap two quickly behind me, I slow my pace back to a jog as I take on lap three. The boy catches up to and passes me. I smile as he sprints by and wonder if we're doing the same patterned running, only on opposite schedules.

We continue on, taking turns passing each other for the next few laps, neither of us saying a word, but we catch each other stealing glances as we pass. He's cute. Really cute. Tall, muscular but lean, sandy blonde hair, a strong jaw— almost a touch too beautiful for my taste, but Ashley would definitely call him hot. I can't imagine many girls wouldn't.

My last lap is a sprinting lap. Only this time, as soon as I pass Hot Boy, he speeds up…and passes me, even though he's not at the point where he is due to switch gears. Keeping a few long strides ahead of me, he maintains his lead for several seconds, until I push myself harder, taking the lead back from him, although not easily. But my position at the front doesn't last long. Hot Boy speeds up and regains the lead. My last lap becomes two laps. Together we run neck and neck, each taking turns edging out the other slightly. Without a doubt it has to be the fastest lap time I've ever run.

Crossing over the finish line, Hot Boy a horse hair before me, we both collapse, struggling to catch our breath. A few minutes later, my breathing finally leveling out, a large hand extends down to help me up. I take it, finally getting a good look at my opponent as he pulls me to my feet. Sparkling blue eyes, a perfectly straight nose and full lips that twitch up on one side steal my barely recovered breath away.

A lopsided, boyish grin forms across his lips and his eyes sweep across my heaving chest. I smile back and, as fast as it came, his smile vanishes. Without a word, he raises a hand, signaling goodbye, turns and takes off, running away from the track.

The entire jog back, I wonder what made his smile disappear so fast.

Chapter 14

Nikki—

Monday

English has always been my favorite subject. After six periods of fidgeting in my chair and being introduced as the new girl, I'm relieved when Mr. Davis just tells me to take a seat and listen. Since it's Honor's English, the class has been grouped together for the last two years while they were sophomores and juniors. It means everyone knows each other very well and I'm truly the new girl. Great.

Mr. Davis reviews the syllabus and holds up our first novel— *The Fault in Our Stars*. I'm excited since it's a novel I've wanted to read. But my excitement is short lived when he tells us the book comes with a group project. The groups are going to be the same as last year, with one exception. Me.

As the bell rings, Mr. Davis yells for me and a student named Allison to stay after class.

"Allison, I thought it might be a good idea for Nikki to join your team for this project. After all, you're down a team member right now since…" he trails off, his voice softer when he continues, "well, you're down a team member right now, Allison."

Allison looks from me to Mr. Davis, and quickly says, "I'm sure he'll be here tomorrow. I thought he'd be here today." She pauses, her voice breaking as she continues, "and I think it might be easier if everything was exactly the same when he comes back. Please," she begs.

Mr. Davis' tone changes from uncomfortable to somber when he replies. "Things aren't going to be the same, Allison."

The two of them stare for a moment. "Fine." Allison finally relents.

I interrupt, "I'll be fine on any team, Mr. Davis. I've read all John Green's other books, so I bet another group would be happy to have me." I definitely don't want to be part of a group where I'm not wanted before we even start.

Mr. Davis and Allison both stare at me with puzzled looks.

"You've read *all* John Green's other books?" Mr. Davis asks with a furrowed brow.

"Do you think people don't read books in Texas?" Insulted, I reply indignantly.

A smile dawns upon Allison's face as I feel my own redden with embarrassment.

"I'm sorry, Nikki. This wasn't about you, or Texas, or even the project. You can be on our team. I welcome the chance to work with someone else who's read all John Green's novels. It's just that Za..," she stops mid-word, shaking her head as if to force her fleeing thought away. "You should be on our team, Nikki. Welcome."

Mr. Davis, satisfied, tells us to run off to lunch before we have no time left to eat.

As we exit Mr. Davis' classroom, Allison says, "Sit at my table for lunch, and we can talk about the project. I'm Allie Parker, by the way."

The cafeteria is five times the size of the one at my last school, and a hell of a lot nicer too. Looking around, I start to dread the thought of Allison Parker dragging me to a table of people I don't know. I can already imagine the snotty, too-pretty-for-their-own-good girls eating tofu and celery sticks so they can fit into their tight, super-short shorts. I spent the first half of this morning in a glass fishbowl office near the front entrance of the school with Aunt Claire and my new guidance counselor. While they talked, and went over my multiple school transcripts, I watched dozens of blonde, heavily made-up, over-dressed girls enter the building. It looked as if a crazy scientist obsessed with Taylor Swift had perfected human cloning and delivered them all to Long Beach High School.

"I usually sit over here." Allie motions to a table that only has a few nerdy looking boys.

I contain my surprise, and give Allie a thorough once over. Her broad smile and pretty face had tricked me into thinking she was a Taylorette. But as I take a closer look, I can see she's a far cry from a clone. Her sweet smile sits on a makeup-free face. True, she has that flawless California tan and great skin, but she's naturally pretty, not primped and polished like the girls I saw this morning. Her clothes are also distinct from those of the clones. Wearing a pair of gray leggings and a long, loose white shirt, she stands apart without clothing clinging to every inch of her body.

Allie takes out a brown paper bag with a peanut butter and jelly sandwich in it, giving me some relief. Aunt Claire packed me a lunch too. I had wondered if I'd be the only one.

We eat lunch quickly, with Allie chattering away about the project and how Mr. Davis runs his class. The period actually flies by as we talk. There's an easy flow to our conversation and I have to remind myself I'm not here to get involved with anything or anyone. I need to keep focused on my goal. I'm here to find my sister.

75

The bell rings, signaling it's time to head to another room of clones. Allie asks for my cell phone number so she can text me about meeting at the library tonight to pick a topic for our literature circle project. I'm embarrassed to tell her that I don't know my own phone number. I've never even held an iPhone until this week, I'm not sure I can figure out how to add a contact quickly. Thinking fast, I hand her my new phone and say, "Here, call yourself on my phone— it's faster." She does and leaves me with a smile and wish of luck for the rest of my classes.

After school, I head out the front doors to look for Aunt Claire. I had told her not to take another day off work, that I could find my way home. If only she knew that I'd moved eight times since grade school, the constant changes leaving me with a better sense of direction than the GPS in her Honda CRV. I've refrained from telling her too much about my life with Mom. She always looks sad when I mention any of our troubles and I don't want anyone's pity.

I survey the line of expensive cars in front of the school, looking for Aunt Claire's Honda. A chill crawls up my spine, raising the tiny hairs on the back of my neck, even though it's almost ninety and there is no breeze. I turn, an eerie feeling of being watched, and scan the area. Nothing is behind me. Nothing to the right. Turning left, I freeze, finding a woman staring at me fixedly. She's just standing there. Alone. Staring. Our eyes lock for a moment. She looks out of place. Her elegant cream-colored suit and two-tone high heels just don't fit in. The teachers dress nice —I learned that today. But not this nice. She doesn't turn away even though I've caught her staring. Oddly, I feel like she's staring, yet doesn't see *me*.

A car horn catches my attention, breaking the pull I feel toward the woman. "Do you know that woman?" I ask as I slide into Aunt Claire's car.

"What woman?"

I look back to where she was just standing, but she's gone. No sign of her anywhere. It's hard to imagine she could disappear so quickly in those heels. "She was standing over there a minute ago." I point toward the tree the woman stood under.

"I only see a bunch of students. What did she look like?"

"I don't know. I guess it was a parent. Maybe she thought she knew me or something." I shrug, feeling silly that I'd even mentioned it. Sometimes I think maybe I inherited Mom's paranoia.

Aunt Claire peppers me with questions about my day. Did I make any friends? Did I like my classes? Did I think the work was the right level? How were the teachers? Did I eat the lunch she'd packed?

I guess she eventually spots my discomfort. "I'm sorry, Nikki. I have to remind myself that you're a high school senior and not a ten year old. I hope I didn't sound like I was trying to mother you too much."

Stopping myself just short of telling her that Mom didn't "mother" the way she thought, I decide to feed her inquisition instead of going down the serious road. "Don't worry about it." I smile halfheartedly. "I think I made a new friend today. Her name is Allie and we're going to be on the same team for an English project. In fact, she asked me to meet the group at the West Long Beach library tonight. Do you know where that is? Can I go?"

Aunt Claire can't hold back her enthusiasm. "Of course you can go. I'm so happy you made a friend. I was worried. This is such a big change for you."

"I know. And thank you." It's not going to be difficult to remember to try to please Aunt Claire so she'll continue to let me stay. She just makes it come naturally.

The library has always been my sanctuary. A place I'd go to escape the reality of my often screwed-up existence. Back in Texas, I'd spend hours alone in the stacks, sitting on the floor flipping through old books, the smell of musty paperbacks strangely comforting— different than the smell of must in our old trailer.

Allie waves to me excitedly from the long table as soon as I walk in, her smile contagious. I'd stood outside a few minutes before coming in, seriously debating on whether or not to go inside. After the long day of firsts, I wasn't sure I was ready for any more. But seeing Allie actually looking happy to see me somehow quells my fear.

"Hey, this is Cory and Keller," Allie says, introducing me to the others already seated at the table. Both look vaguely familiar. I must have seen them in English class today, but after taking in a thousand new faces, I'm a bit too overwhelmed to remember much about any single person.

It takes less than three minutes sitting at the table, before the group dynamic is clear. Keller Daughtry looks like a linebacker, an intimidating one. I wouldn't be surprised if he growled instead of spoke. He's broad and muscular, with short, cropped hair and loads of bite in everything he says. But it's the kind of sarcastic wit that's said with a grin, and the group looks like they enjoy poking the lion almost as much as he enjoys delivering the lashing. Cory is the quiet one of the trio. She smiles and laughs, taking in the exchanges among the group rather than jumping into the middle.

"So what's your story?" Keller asks, bending back his chair on its hind legs, his arms folded over his chest.

"My story?" I know what he's asking, yet the question catches me off guard.

"Yeah. You know, where'd you move from? You play any sports? Is Allie going to have to carry your ass in this project too, like she does mine?" Keller shrugs. "Your story."

All eyes turn to me. I do my best to feign casual, even though I'm anything but comfortable talking about *my story*. "Ummm…I moved here from Texas. I ran track at school. And I hope Allison doesn't have to carry me." Keller watches me intently, unsure what to make of what he sees, so, without thinking, I let who I am slip out to show him. Arching one eyebrow, I intentionally graze my eyes across the girth of him before I speak. "I'm not sure she can carry my ass, since she's probably already suffocating under the weight of yours."

Keller throws his head back and laughs. "You're going to fit right in, although I'm not sure I can put up with another smartass in the group."

We discuss our project choices until a little before the library closes, the hours passing more like minutes. Allie has a passion for reading that brings everyone into the story, even Keller, who I get the feeling isn't always the greatest student.

Allie and I talk for a few minutes out front as I wait for my aunt. "So, you run track?"

"Yeah, you?"

She laughs. "Definitely not. I run like a duck. Running isn't my thing. I played soccer for a little while when I was a kid. My dad really wanted a jock. With two girls, luckily my little brother came along and it took some of the pressure off us. I try to stick to sports that don't entail running." She pauses, then adds, "Zack runs track."

"Your brother?" I ask with a furrowed brow.

"No. Zack's the other person in our group." She looks at me blankly for a second. "He plays football too."

"Oh. Is he sick or something?" The minute the question leaves my mouth, Allie's face changes. Sadness covers her usually sunny smile. I immediately regret asking the question.

She attempts to recover her smile, but fails to make it even slightly believable. "I'm hoping he comes back soon."

Aunt Claire couldn't have better timing as she pulls up, I'd stuck my foot in my mouth enough for one day.

Chapter 15

Zack—

Wednesday

I knew it was coming before my parents sat me down. It was only a matter of time. I was out of school the last few months after Emily died and then a whole summer passed. I think Mom and Dad were afraid to argue with me yesterday, when I said I wasn't going for the first day of school, but they aren't going to let this go any further— at least that's what I overheard Dad saying to Mom after dinner. So tonight, they pulled the plug on my avoidance. Tomorrow is going to suck.

Rather than try to spend time convincing them that I should stay home, I decide to go for a run. I've been running a lot lately. Music blaring in my ears, feet pounding hard on the concrete beneath my feet, nothing else seems to clear my head. I take the new route I've been tracking, unable to bring myself to follow any of the paths that Emily and I usually ran. I slow as I reach the library. Allie's car is outside. So is Keller's. I've felt guilty about the way I spoke to her the night she came to see me. She was only trying to

81

help. She's texted me a few times since then, but I didn't answer any of the texts. The only ones I've returned were a few of Keller's, because I knew he would show up if I didn't.

Instead of continuing on my run, I take a deep breath, lower the volume on my iPod, wipe the sweat from my brow and make my way into the library.

They're at our usual table. Allie's back is to me, so she doesn't see my approach, but Keller nods in my direction, a guy greeting of hello.

"Hey." I say, my voice directed at no one in particular. Allie turns. Her eyes go wide, but she attempts to come off casual.

"Hey. You're here?" She smiles hesitantly.

"Actually, I was just on a run and saw your cars parked outside. I'm sort of too sweaty to sit down and join in, but thought I'd say hi. Pretty sure I'm coming to school tomorrow." Not by choice, but I leave that part out.

"Sorry, I'm late," an unfamiliar girl's voice says from behind me. She walks to the table hurriedly, tossing her bag onto the table and pulls out a chair. Never looking up, she digs into her backpack, searching for something. Distracted, she doesn't notice me standing here, but hell, I notice her.

As soon as I see her face, I know who she is…the girl from the track. I'm curious for her to look up so I can get a better view, but I'm also glad to have a minute to stare without being noticed. She's beautiful, although not in the typical California girl sense. Fair skin, a thin, straight nose, full pink lips and dark blonde hair that makes her untanned skin stand out in contrast to the golden California girls all the more.

Sensing my staring, she looks up, our eyes connecting immediately. It takes her less than two heartbeats before recognition kicks in. Her mouth parts on a sharp inhale. It's odd, I've avoided eye contact for months now, yet I'm glued to her, unable to tear away my gaze.

Not unlike our first meeting, neither of us say a word. Only this time, she turns it into a challenge. She arches one eyebrow, a small twitch at the corner of her mouth telling me she's amused with our muted exchanges.

"Zack?" Allie says, confusion evident in her voice. I hear her words, but the fact that she's calling my name, trying to get my attention, doesn't really register with me. "Zack," She calls a second time, the confusion in her voice changing to concern. It snaps me out of my fog and I turn, begrudgingly breaking our gaze.

"So do you think you'll be able to come?" Allie eyes me up and down as if to make sure I'm okay.

I furrow my brow. She's completely unaware that I haven't heard a word she's said the last few minutes.

"The Grind. Tomorrow night," she repeats. "The library closes early and we're going to work on the project ."

I nod. Feeling eyes on me, I turn my attention back to the girl from the track. I wasn't wrong, she's watching me…closely too. Allie catches my attention shift.

"This is Nikki," she says, "she's new at LBH. Mr. Davis assigned her to our group."

I extend my hand, but say nothing, letting the smirk on my face do all the talking. Nikki puts her hand in mine and smiles back with a nod. We've got some sort of an unspoken challenge going, neither of us wanting to be the first to speak. It's bizarre since I've never really met the girl, but I realize, as I shake her hand longer than would be considered normal, that I've smiled twice in the last few weeks. Both times around her.

The first half of the run back home, I contemplate the oddness of my behavior. Why had I suddenly become mute around a strange girl? Sure, she's pretty, there's no denying it, but there's something more. I'm drawn to her. When I look into her eyes, see the smirk on her face, I don't feel the anger that bogs me down around everyone else. Maybe it's because she's new…there's no reminder of the life I want to escape so badly. I'm not sure, but a vision of her keeps popping back into my head with every step. And it makes me feel guilty. God I'm such an asshole. My girlfriend is gone barely six months and I'm already checking out replacements.

I run faster and faster, desperate to make the feelings go away. The ones that make me feel good cause me more pain than the ones that torment me. At least I deserve the torment, I don't deserve to feel good.

Chapter 16

Nikki

"It's about time!" Ashley calls at midnight, yelling so loud that I pull the cellphone away from my ear. It's only been a few days, but since the first day we became friends we definitely haven't gone this long without speaking.

"Sorry. I've been so busy."

"Doing what? Or should I say whom?" she teases. I flop down on my bed and close my eyes, envisioning Ashley grinning and wiggling her eyebrows suggestively. I bet she's lying belly-down on her bed, legs flailing in the air as we talk.

I sigh and tell her about my first few days at LBH, filling her in on my classes and track tryouts, but that's not what she's interested in.

"Blah, blah, blah…trigonometry, running in circles…tell that crap to your Aunt Claire. I want to hear the juicy stuff." Ashley says, only half joking.

"There's not really any juicy stuff to tell." I pause. "Except…"

"Tell me," Ashley demands.

"There really isn't anything to tell."

"There's something." She knows me so well.

"Well, I met a cute guy," I confess.

Ashley squeals in response. "Describe him. I'm going to close my eyes…give me the visual."

I close mine too. A picture of Zack pops into my head without even having to take the time to think about him. That's been happening a lot lately. "Well, he's tall…maybe six feet."

"Mmmmm…tall's good. Go on."

"Broad shouldered. Lean, but muscular."

"Sounds yummy. Eyes?"

"Yes, he has two of them."

"Smartass."

"Blue with a hint of green. The color of Caribbean water."

"You've never been to the Caribbean."

"Shut up."

"Go on."

"Nice lips. Full."

"Mmmmm," Ashley groans at the visual I'm painting for her. "More."

"Dimples. He has dimples. And he doesn't even have to smile to show them…he just sort of smirks and they appear."

"He sounds perfect." She exhales loudly before adding, "For me."

I can't help but giggle at her reply. Though I know she'd never go for the same boy as me, even if we were still in the same school. She likes boys she meets in detention, like Tommy Damon who smokes pot under the bleachers alongside the track…not the boys that run on it.

"Is his voice sexy? I like a deep voice. A guy who squeaks my name ruins it for me. Totally."

"I don't know."

"You haven't spoken to him?" she asks, confused.

"Nope."

"I thought you said you met him."

"I did."

"Is he mute?"

"Maybe," I tease, resting my chin in my hands as I prop up my head while still lying on my belly, diagonally across the bed.

"So you're hot for him, but you've never spoken to him?"

"I didn't say I was hot for him," I respond, a bit too defensively for her statement to be wrong.

"You're hot for him," she insists.

"Ugh," I groan. "I don't know why I tell you anything."

"Because I'm awesome at giving fishing advice."

"Fishing advice?"

"Yeah…I'm going to tell you exactly how to bait the hook and reel him in."

Day four of school and I'm finally getting the layout of the building, actually making it to English before the bell rings for the first time. Allie is busy provoking Keller as I walk over and take the seat behind her and across from our other two team members.

"I'm a vegan, I don't consume animal protein," Allie says with a flick of her wrist, dismissing whatever Keller has just suggested.

"So? They have chicken."

Allie's eyes bulge in disbelief. "Chicken is animal protein!"

"No chicken?" Keller looks appalled at the thought.

The two continue on while I set my backpack on the floor, head down searching for my textbook. Of course, it's all the way down at the bottom of my bag and I need to unpack everything to get to it. I make a mental note to figure out a packing regimen that will work for my class schedule.

Abruptly, the class goes quiet, a few whispers replacing the loud chatter from just minutes before. I look up, expecting to see Mr. Davis has just entered the room. But instead I find Zack.

He doesn't do anything for a minute while he looks around the room. His jaw clenches as he takes in all the eyes locked on him. For a second I think he's going to turn back around and leave, but Mr. Davis walks in, oblivious to whatever is going on, and tells everyone to take a seat.

Allie lifts her hand and quietly calls to Zack, pointing to an empty seat across from her. Begrudgingly, he takes the seat, never looking up again.

Mr. Davis wastes no time jumping right in. "Alright everyone, take out a sheet of paper and a pencil."

There's some grumbling, but a minute later, everyone is ready. Everyone except Zack, that is. It looks like he doesn't have anything to write with. He turns to the guy in the row on the other side of him and mumbles something. The guy shakes his head. Then he turns in my direction. Mouth poised to say something, most likely to ask for a pencil, he looks up and stops short before speaking. For a second, I see what I think might be a flash of attraction in his eyes, but it's quickly extinguished. Instead, he looks down for a moment, regrouping, then back up at me, a glint of amusement in his eyes. Pursing his lips together, he motions with his hand, pretending to write in the air, a wordless game of charades.

I can't hide my smile as I extend a pencil in his direction with only a nod and a grin.

Mr. Davis doesn't waste any time beginning his lecture. Today we're going to discuss the summer reading assignment, *Wuthering Heights*. He asks for a show of hands to see how many have actually read the book. Just about everyone raises their hands. Everyone except Zack. Somehow, it seems unlikely that every senior has done the summer reading. The reality is probably that Zack is the only one brave enough to admit he hasn't.

I do my best to concentrate on the lecture, but my eyes keep wandering back to Zack. He's seated across from me, but one seat up, so it's easy for me to steal glances without being caught. He's wearing jeans and a plain black t-shirt, dark sneakers...very simple, yet sexy at the same time. Only, it's not the outfit that does it, it's the way he wears it, fitting snugly across his wide shoulders, the sleeves yielding tightly to the thickness of his arms. Somehow it doesn't seem like he's trying to look good, or even knows that he does.

His sandy blonde hair is messy; it looks as if his idea of styling it might have been to run his fingers through it in frustration, daring it to move out of place. It's longish, the back hitting almost to the collar of his shirt. He could probably use a cut, but the unstyled, just-out-of-bed look only adds to his sex appeal.

Instead of paying attention, he alternates between staring off into space and doodling something on the paper. I can't distinguish if his lack of attention is from boredom with the teacher or distraction because of something else all together.

Realizing I'm spending way too much time watching someone I shouldn't be focused on, I force my attention back to the teacher, deciding to write notes as he talks in order to occupy my eyes. But it doesn't take long before my mind starts wandering again, seeing as I've read this story and analyzed it ad nauseum in my advanced English class last year. Of course, my eyes can't help but follow my mind. Only this time, when I find myself staring, watching the boy who looks as distracted as I feel, Zack turns and catches me.

Crap.

My first reaction is to look away quickly, as though if I did it fast enough he wouldn't think I was staring. Stupidly, I look up a few seconds later to see if he's bought what I'm trying to pass off as a casual glance of chance, rather than stalkerish staring, and I find he's staring back at me. Intently.

My eyes react automatically by looking away again, but they quickly make their way back, getting caught in his gaze. It's just so direct and attentive. My heart speeds up and I feel my face heat with embarrassment as my eyes flicker back and forth to his, trying to decide what to do. Not nearly as uncomfortable with our direct stare, Zack's still not turning away. No, instead, the corner of his mouth twitches toward a grin. He's relishing my discomfort at being caught.

Luckily, the bell rings and Allie turns to talk to me, completely oblivious to the tension she is breaking. I grab my books and pack up quickly as she talks, needing to put some distance between me and the voiceless boy.

"We're going to work on our project tonight, 6pm. I'll pick you up so your Aunt doesn't have to drive you. Text me your address," Allie instructs and I agree.

I glance back in Zack's direction, only to find his seat vacant. He's disappeared as wordlessly as he arrived. Looking down, I find a folded-up note propped on my desk, *Thanks for the pencil.*

Chapter 17

Zack

This time tomorrow we'll both be different. Tonight's a night we'll never forget. I can't wait. XO Em. Sitting in my room, the post-it-note I'd found stuck to my dashboard the morning of the bonfire clutched in my hand, my mind wanders to Nikki today in class. The way she looked at me, her big green eyes and pale skin, skin that betrays her as it flushes at being caught. There's just something about her that I'm drawn to, something that makes me smile when everything else around me only makes me angry.

Lost in thought for a few seconds, I grimace when I look down and see Emily's handwriting. Guilt sickens me. I should be picturing Emily. I read the note for the thousandth time. *This time tomorrow we'll both be different. Tonight's a night we'll never forget. I can't wait. XO Em.* I shut my eyes and will my mind to see Emily. Nikki's green eyes greet me.

Again. *This time tomorrow we'll both be different. Tonight's a night we'll never forget. I can't wait. XO Em.* Eyes closed tightly, I try to remember Emily on that last day — the last time she smiled, the last time she was happy. Instead, the curve of Nikki's mouth fills my subconscious.

I hate myself. Again. *This time tomorrow we'll both be different. Tonight's a night we'll never forget. I can't wait. XO Em.* I squeeze my eyes shut tighter. Again. *This time tomorrow we'll both be different. Tonight's a night we'll never forget. I can't wait. XO Em.* Twenty more tries are no more successful than my first attempt. My eyes jar open, leaving Nikki's face behind. I shred the note into a hundred tiny pieces.

The door to my room creaks open loudly. My mother knocks softly even though she's already opened the door. "Zack."

I don't respond.

"Sweetie." Her tone is soft, pensive. I feel badly for making her walk on eggshells, but I don't know how to get myself back to where I was. I'm not sure if I can ever go back. Too much has changed. I've changed.

She sits down next to me on the bed. I crumple the little yellow post-it pieces into my hand. Mom takes her hand and covers mine, the one clutching Emily's note.

"I thought you were going to work on your English project tonight?"

"Changed my mind," I say tersely. I don't really feel like debating my social life, or lack thereof.

"Why?" Why the hell does she think? I don't respond, not because I have nothing to say, but because she won't like what she hears.

"Zack?" Her voice rises to that motherly tone. The one that's a warning more than a question. I stare at her blankly, but she doesn't back down.

"Go. You need to get out. You need to be around some friends. Work on your project. You always feel good around Keller. Go."

Annoyed at her persistence, I stand. Wadding up the torn Post-It in my hand, I peg it at the garbage can in the corner of my room. I miss, but don't bother to pick up the tiny, yellow pieces scattered all over the floor on my way out. I slam the door behind me.

With no destination in mind, I drive around aimlessly for more than an hour. It's nearly nine when I arrive at The Grind, the coffee shop I was supposed to meet the group at. Allie's red Volkswagen is parked right out front, the hood open as she and Keller peer into the engine. I pull over because, even though I choose to wallow in my own self pity, I'm not that big of a dick that I'd pass a friend who looks like they could use a hand.

"Zack," Allie says as she sees me approach. "You're about three hours late." Unlike most everyone else around me, she'll call me on my shit, instead of tiptoeing like I'm fragile and might break.

I smile and shake my head. "Thanks. I thought I was right on time," I reply, equally sarcastic. "What's going on?"

"It won't start."

"What happens when you turn the key?"

"Not much, it makes a click-click sound." Keller shrugs.

"Turn it...let me hear." Allie walks around to the driver's side, gets in and tries to start it.

"It's the starter." Years of working on old cars with my dad, I've picked up on some of the common car repairs.

"That's what my dad said."

I nod. "Is he coming for you?"

"Yeah. But he's coming straight from work and he's got his little two-seater, divorced-on-the-prowl car, so I can't give Nikki and Keller a ride home."

"Nikki?" I look around.

"She just went inside to use the ladies room. Here she comes now." Allie points just as Nikki walks through the front door and our eyes meet.

"I can give them a ride."

"That would be great."

Allie's father pulls up in his two-seater Porsche just as Nikki makes her way back over to us. She smiles at me and I smile back.

"Did you call your Aunt already?" Keller asks.

She shakes her head no.

"Good. Zack's going to give us a lift."

Chapter 18

Nikki

Keller's house is only a few blocks from The Grind. As we pull up, Zack hops out with Keller. The two exchange a few words I can't hear, and then Zack opens the door to the back seat, offering his hand for me to get out. The other hand reaches forward and opens the front passenger door. He waits until I'm inside to close it, then jogs around to the other side.

His right hand on the gear shifter, for a second it looks like he's going to drive, but then he changes his mind. Leaving the car in park, he turns to face me. Lifting one knee up onto the seat and twisting his body toward me, he slings one arm casually around the back of the seat. It's just the two of us in the car now and suddenly the inside of the spacious car seems smaller. Maybe even a little warmer.

He looks at me and arches an eyebrow with a grin. Although fully aware I need to give him my aunt's address, I play along. Grinning back, I arch an eyebrow in return and fold my arms stubbornly over my chest.

Throwing his head back, Zack laughs. The deep, raspy sound echoes through me, the sound warming me. It befits his handsome face. Together we have a good chuckle and then he extends his hand to me and through a sexy half smile, I finally hear his voice, "Zack Martin."

I oblige. "Nikki Fallon."

"Nice to finally meet you, Nikki Fallon." He doesn't let go of my hand as he speaks.

"You too." I feel the warmth from his hand spread through me.

"I was beginning to think you were mute."

My eyes widen. "Me? You're the one who started this."

"I haven't been much of a talker lately, I guess." He opens his mouth as if to say something else, then shuts it.

I shrug, completely understanding how he feels, although I'm sure for different reasons. "I get it. Sometimes you just don't feel like talking. Lately I feel like every word I say is analyzed for a hidden meaning."

Zack releases my hand and instantly I feel the warmth that had spread through my whole body start to cool. As he turns back to face the road, I shiver from the sudden temperature change.

"Cold, in this weather?" he asks with surprise as he shifts the car into gear.

I'm not going to tell him that my body temperature dropped drastically when he let go of my hand. I blush just thinking about how hot my body had become just from the feeling of his hand in mine.

"Not cold, just a little shiver, it happens to me sometimes." As if I have a medical condition and it's not the result of hormones surging through my seventeen-year-old body.

"Yeah, women always have that problem around me," Zack teases, glancing my way. I see a flicker in his eyes. It's there. There's some spark that neither of us are quite comfortable with. But we also can't seem to stop fanning the fire.

"On second thought, I think I'm cold." A little smirk appears between his two delicious dimples.

"Where to?" Zack asks, looking straight ahead at the road. Is he trying to avoid another meeting of our eyes?

"Uhm. I don't know. I, uh…" Nervously, I try to respond with coherent words but fail. He wants to take me somewhere?

"You don't know where you live, silly?" Zack mocks with a now broad smile, which splatters warmth across the cool bucket seats and stirs some embarrassing sensations throughout my body.

I try to will away the redness I know is glowing in my otherwise pale cheeks. "I thought you could figure that out without any words, Zack Martin, the Wordless Wonder."

"I knew you thought I was a wonder." He's unquestionably enjoying our banter.

Before I can respond, Zack turns onto my street and is slowing right before Aunt Claire's house.

"Stalk people much?" I exclaim, genuinely surprised he already knows where I live.

"You always have to wonder about the quiet ones, Nikki. Always." Zack sneaks in one last dazzling smile before he turns to open his door.

When he appears at the passenger door and reaches in to help me out of the car, my legs instantly turn to Jell-O. Zack grabs my hand to help me out, and the combination of my unsteady legs and the heady feeling his touch brings me causes me to miss my step. I stumble and fall right into his arms.

"Whoa, are you okay?" Zack laughs but keeps his arms around me as he looks down to make sure I really am okay.

Thank god it's dark, because I have never felt this flushed in my life. I'm taken aback by my body's reaction to the feel of his arms wrapped around me. Does he sense it too? Surely, he must know what his nearness is doing to me.

I look up to profess my clumsiness and our eyes meet…closer…much closer than before. Zack suddenly straightens and steadies me on my feet. "Do you need me to walk you to the front door?" There's a sudden and severe change in his body language and a flatness in his voice. He may as well be asking an old lady if she needs help crossing the street.

"I'm fine. Just a little clumsy. You can go." My hurt feelings are evident in my words and surely on my face. I've never been good at hiding my hurt.

Zack doesn't seem to notice though. He's already disappeared mentally, if not physically. "See you in school," His voice is mechanical, without any hint of the playful guy who was flirting with me just moments ago. He doesn't even look back as he walks away.

Zack, his well-bred manners intact, sits in the car watching to assure I make it into Aunt Claire's house safely. As soon I close the door behind me, he pulls away from the curb. Watching out the window, I'm reminded of the way his demeanor changed at the track. What is it that enters Zack's head and robs that flicker from his beautiful eyes?

Later that night, I toss and turn, unable to sleep, remembering the surge of heat that flushed through my body at Zack's touch. I don't ever remember feeling anything like it before. As much as I know I need to stay focused on why I came to Long Beach to begin with, it's pretty impossible to erase the feeling from my mind. Or body.

As I fall asleep, I start thinking about my sister. Until I met Ashley, I never had anyone to share my most personal thoughts with. Mom and I didn't have that kind of relationship. I wouldn't have told her about Zack. At least I don't think so. But, a sister… a sister is exactly who you would share this stuff with. Perhaps mine is popular and has had boyfriends— she'll have all the right advice .

Zack

As I walk in the front door of our house, I realize I don't even remember the drive home from Nikki's. That happens a lot lately. Minutes, hours and days disappear. I'm alive, but I'm not really living. It's what I deserve. I don't deserve to feel. Not when Emily can't anymore.

But being near Nikki *makes* me feel. It's not just in my head either. It's physical too. A draw, a pull, an energy that zaps me back from the land of numb. Even the slightest touch, a simple handshake, brings me back to life. Sure I remember the excitement of being around Emily. The ache in my groin just from a glimpse of her in a bikini. But I don't remember this. When Nikki tripped out of the car tonight, my legs went so weak at the touch of her body that I almost fell myself. What the fuck is wrong with me?

I toss and turn all night trying to stop feeling, but the emotions are just too powerful. I shower for school the next morning, reasoning with myself that all I need to do is stay away from her. If I don't touch, the feeling won't come back. It should be simple.

It saddens me that nothing seems to have changed, yet everything is different. The numbness I wanted so desperately last night found me the moment I walked into school. Maybe it was the sight of a gaggle of girls in the courtyard who reminded me of Emily. Beautiful bodies dressed to perfection, outlined with golden hair. Poised for viewing. The courtyard was Emily's favorite place to show off her runway outfits.

Walking into school doesn't get easier with each day that passes. Dad said it would and so did the leader of the support group Mom and Dad made me go to every week all summer. But they're wrong. They're all wrong.

It happens again as I walk into Mr. Davis's class. I realize the walk between the courtyard and class is lost. But when I walk into English, I'm pulled back by the sight of Nikki. The only open desk in the room is directly behind her. She looks down into her notebook, seemingly so unaffected by everyone around her...guys showing off, girls carrying on about their ridiculously overpriced shoes.

I inhale a deep breath and walk to the desk. I almost make it past her when she looks up and spots me. I recognize the expression on her face. She doesn't know how to react to my presence. It's an expression I'm way too familiar with the last few months.

Allie either doesn't notice or ignores my brooding. "Hey Zack. Thanks for driving Keller and Nikki home last night. My car is out of commission for now."

"No problem," I mumble as I take the seat behind Nikki and next to Allie.

Keller slams his body into the seat on the other side of me. "Coach said you better show up at football practice today if you want to play at homecoming." He tries to sound like he's just delivering a message, but it's also his own curiosity wanting to know if I'm coming back to the team.

"I've only missed a few days," I snap back at him.

"A few days *and* the entire summer," he quickly reminds me. "If it was anyone else he wouldn't even let them play. But I think he's serious. You better come to practice today."

Nikki looks up from her notes with a strain of her eyes to pay attention. Our eyes meet and she looks away quickly. There's no smile on her face. I need to see it, be the one to put it there.

Trying to make light and ease the tension in the air, I respond to Keller but look at Nikki, "I might just have to come back to the team. Poor Nikki shouldn't have to watch you try and play quarterback at homecoming. It wouldn't be fair to our new classmate."

Nikki turns toward me, a smile lighting her face. And there it is again— that feeling of being alive.

The next forty minutes of English fly by while I examine Nikki from behind. Not the kind of *from behind* most guys want to examine. Instead I watch her hair sway across her shoulders as she moves back and forth in her seat. She seems almost restless, barely able to sit still.

I think about saying something to her directly as we exit class, but Keller intercepts the opportunity, his large frame blocking my way. Still waiting for a real answer from me, he won't relent.

"I'll take it easy on you at practice. Don't want to hurt you, being that you're so out of shape and all," Keller baits me.

"Take it easy on me? You're the one who's out of shape, buddy." As we walk down the hallway, I knock him gently into the lockers alongside him.

Keller recovers and returns the shove, grinning. "That pretty boy face is going to wind up bruised if you try that again." It's a threat, but there's nothing but pleasure in this voice.

A few other members of the team catch up to the two of us. All week, the halls have been brimming with talk of homecoming and the big game, and today is no different. Football player egos crowd the halls just as I veer off toward my next class.

"See you at practice," Keller yells after me with conviction, as I disappear into chemistry.

He just might.

Zack

Dirt cakes the legs of my once white practice pants, I've been knocked on my ass more in the last hour than I have been in the last two seasons. *What the fuck?*

Keller extends a large hand down to help me up for what is probably the tenth time. "Dude, get your head out of your ass or Coach is going to bench you."

"Screw you," I spit back.

He smirks, always the wise ass, "You're pretty, but not my type. I like bigger titties." He holds his cupped hands to his chest, making the universal guy sign for large breasts.

"You're an idiot." He is, but I say it in jest, the anger of being knocked on my ass, repeatedly, disappearing easier than it should. I'm physically present, but something is missing.

"I'm not the one who can't figure out how to throw the ball or move out of the way of the two-hundred-pound guy charging at me. Your feet turn to lead or something? Maybe you need to take some ballet lessons to limber up…you know, with the other girls?"

"Fuck you," I grunt with a smile he can't see under my helmet, yet I'm sure he knows it's there.

"Speaking of fucking..." Keller trails off as we line up into T formation, his head nods in the direction of a few of the girls from track running a relay race. I look without interest. Until I see *her*.

Keller, my center that had filled in as quarterback in my absence, snaps the ball into my hands. I'm completely unprepared, my eyes still on Nikki's long lean legs, as the opposing players pummel me yet again.

"Hey, quarterback, you gonna join us anytime soon?" Coach Callihan yells impatiently at me.

Picking myself up off the ground yet again, I spit dirt— mixed with a little blood from my rapidly swelling lip— before I respond, "Maybe if I could get a little help from the offensive line, I might be able to stand long enough to stretch out my arm to throw the ball." I know my putting blame on someone else won't sit well with Coach, but I don't give a shit.

"That just bought you eight laps *with* equipment on. Everyone else, hit the showers. We're going to have to start extra early tomorrow. 6.AM. You can all thank Mr. Martin for the pre-dawn Saturday morning practice."

The team groans, a few even mumble something about me being an asshole under their breath, but no one complains to Coach. No one is stupid enough. Ripping my helmet from my head, I toss it on the ground, readying myself for my eight-lap, big-mouth punishment.

"Hang on a minute, Martin." Coach Callihan strides toward me. "Son." He puts a hand on my padded shoulder. "I know you've had a tough year. But this isn't a sport you can do without your head in the game. You're liable to get hurt." He looks me in the eye, waiting for something— perhaps it's my response he expects— but I just stare back blankly. After a minute, his face changes. It's clear something's dawned on him. He lowers his voice from stern to almost fatherly. "You don't care if you get hurt, do you?"

By lap seven, my legs start to burn. Between getting knocked around at practice and running with an extra ten pounds of equipment on me, I feel pain in every stride. The track team ended practice fifteen minutes ago, leaving me nothing to take my mind off my aching body anymore.

As I cross the start line to begin my last lap, I feel the pounding of footsteps from behind me before I even see her. Falling into sync with my slow pace, Nikki says, "Race a lap, slowpoke?"

My faltering gait comes to life. "Races have winners. Winners get a prize. What are we betting?" I throw her a devilish grin, trying to cover up how winded I really am.

Nikki's mouth twists as she ponders, unsure of how to respond. "How about, loser buys the winner's lunch Monday at school?"

"Lunch? Nah. That's not a big enough prize." My heart beats a little faster. "Dinner."

"Okay, but I'm ordering the most expensive thing on the menu." Nikki takes off like a bat out of hell. The girl runs like the wind— she's a half dozen steps ahead of me before I even realize we've started.

Forcing one leg in front of the other, I try my damnedest to catch up to her, but I just don't have it in me after seven long laps. Halfway through, it dawns on me…why am I even trying? I lose, I get to buy her dinner. I jog the last half of the track, enjoying the view from the rear.

Winded from her lightning speed sprint, Nikki bends over, hands on her hips. "Did you even *try* to win?"

"Nope," I respond unapologetically, reaching down for my water bottle. I spray half into my mouth and the rest over my sweaty head. The padding and uniform, mixed with the unusually high temperature, leaves me feeling like I just ran two miles in a heated blanket.

"I won the bet fair and square, even if you decided not to try to win."

"I'm not a welcher. Dinner's on me."

Nikki's aunt is waiting for her across the parking lot, so we say goodbye and I head for the locker room. Most of the team is gone by the time I hit the shower, except Keller, who waited, knowing I'd drive him home.

"You and Nikki?" he questions as I dry off.

I know what he's asking, but I make him spell it out anyway. "Me and Nikki what?"

"Together?"

"No." My response is curt.

"She's fucking hot. Did you see her ass in those tight little running shorts?" Keller asks with a dirty grin on his face. One I get the urge to smack off immediately.

"You're a dick. You know that?"

"Yeah, and you know it too. Big deal." He shrugs, not the slightest bit put off by being called a dick. In fact, I think he wears the title like a badge of honor. "So, you don't care if I ask her to the dance then?"

My blood instantly boils. A possessiveness I'm not entitled to have grips me. "Whatever." I slam my locker door.

"Cool." Keller walks away whistling, enjoying he's gotten under my skin.

I don't say more than two words on the drive home. I hate myself for wanting it to be me to ask her to the dance.

Nikki

"**D**amn it!" Startled by the vibration of my iPhone in my pocket, I jump from the desk chair in Aunt Claire's office. More than a dozen manila folders spill from my arms and splatter onto the floor. Loose papers scatter from neatly labeled files. I'll never be able to put everything back in the order Aunt Claire had them in. Files with tax returns, receipts, insurance papers, and medical invoices line the floor. Nothing even remotely related to me, or my sister. Not even a single paper about Mom.

I do my best to replace the papers in the right files and alphabetize the folders before dropping them back into the wooden filing cabinet. Aunt Claire is a lot more organized than Mom ever was. Mom's idea of filing was tossing crumpled papers into a shoebox under the bed.

Discouraged after yet another fruitless search, I pick up the phone to call Ashley back.

"It's about time. Thought I was going to have to hitch all the way to sunny ass California," Ashley answers on the first ring. I hear loud music blaring in the background.

"Where are you?"

"Texas," she responds and I can hear the smile in her voice.

"Obviously. But where...there's music blasting in the background."

She laughs. The music becomes more distant as she continues; she must be walking away for privacy. "Down at the lake."

"Oh." A vision of Caddo Lake fills my mind. The tall, moss-draped cypress trees and lush green vegetation surround the massive deep blue water, making it appear fantasy like. Almost like it's part of a Louisiana swamp instead of the Texas national forest system. Ash and I used to spend hours down there swimming in a secluded area. Selfishly, it makes me sad that she's there with someone else, instead of me.

She picks up on my feeling, even though we're separated by two states and I've only said a half dozen words. It makes me miss her even more.

"You're not missing much. Sean Drexler just ripped apart our favorite place to sit with his dirt bike. Our little green grass patch under the big tree is now a mud patch."

"Sean Drexler? Nick's older brother? You're down at the lake with Sean?"

"Don't worry, mother hen...there's a bunch of us, not just the two of us."

I sigh. "I feel like you're cheating on me, going to our spot with other people."

"Ummm...hello. I had to come down with *six* people to replace one of you, and it's still not as much fun."

I'm sure she's lying, Sean and Nick are crazy. It would be nearly impossible to not have a good time hanging around with them. But it makes me feel better nonetheless.

"So, any leads on your sister?" Ashley asks, turning our light conversation serious, her voice dips with the mood.

"No," I say, deflated. "I've searched almost the entire house. Every time Aunt Claire leaves, I snoop around more— but I haven't found anything, really. Although, I did find out a little about California law on the internet. Since we were born in California, the adoption was most likely done here. And in California, a person can find out identifying information on their biological siblings at age eighteen."

"That's great! You don't have long to go then."

"Yes, but what if she's, you know…like my mother?"

"Crazy?"

"Not crazy! Bipolar!" I reprimand Ashley's loose terminology, even though I know she means no harm.

"Whatever. If she's a bat loon, then you pack up your stuff and come back to Texas and live with me."

"You know your mom wouldn't be able to take me in permanently."

"Who said anything about Mom? We turn eighteen within a few weeks of each other. We can go down to Padre Island, get a cheap place to live and waitress or something," Ashley says it like it's no big deal. I actually picture her shrugging after she finishes her declaration. Funny enough, for Ashley it really *is* something she could easily do. I'm the one who needs the plan, the backup plan and the backup to the backup plan.

"Sounds good. How are you getting through English without me?"

"It went from being my easiest subject to my hardest since you left."

"That's because you copied all of my homework and sat next to me for the tests," I tease, although it's true.

"So how is mute hot guy?"

"He talks now."

"And…"

I sigh loudly as I roll onto my back on the bed. "Even his voice is sort of hot."

"You got it bad if you think his voice is hot!" Ashley laughs.

"It's not so much his voice, but how he says things. I can't explain it. He has a quiet confidence about him, he doesn't really ask when he wants something, he just sort of tells you with a crooked grin."

"*You* like a bossy pants? I can't believe it...I thought opposites attracted."

"Hey!" I feign offense. "I'm not bossy. And he's not a bossy pants...it's more like a confidence."

"Whatever. Does he know you like him?" she asks.

"I don't know. He's hard to read. Sometimes I think he does, and that he sort of likes me too. But then other times he just looks at me differently. Sort of blankly...like I'm not even there."

"Hmmm...sounds like a catch."

"Shut up!" I yell through my laughter.

"Maybe you should just jump his bones?"

"Great advice, coming from the girl with less experience than me."

"I don't have less experience than you. I have the same barely-worth-mentioning experience as you."

We talk on the phone for another twenty minutes, catching up about school and our plans for after graduation. I tell her about my bet with Zack and how we're meeting tonight, a few hours before our group is getting together to work on our project. He's paying off his bet with a dinner at Meson Ole, his favorite Mexican restaurant. Before we hang up, Ashley tells me that, tomorrow, she's going to put flowers on Mom's grave for me.

"You remembered."

"Of course I did." We're both silent for a minute. "Remember the time your mom tried to make teal cupcakes to match my hair for my fifteenth birthday? She decorated the entire trailer in teal crepe paper too? But the cupcakes turned out grey and the crepe paper stayed up for four months and then she announced it was an Easter decoration."

I smile thinking of Ashley passing the gross cupcakes out to the neighbors after mom went to sleep, so we could pretend we ate them all.

"How could I forget?"

That was one of her manic periods, when mom was happy and liked to throw little parties for us. Mom had remembered Ashley's birthday, but her own mother hadn't.

A tear creeps down my cheek. Life was good. I had Mom and she had me. And I was lucky enough to find a friend like Ash.

"You look very pretty." I come down the stairs a few minutes before Zack is due to pick me up. Aunt Claire spots me from the kitchen as she wipes down the counters.

"Thank you."

"Cute boy in your project group?" She smiles, fishing for the reason why I've done my hair and makeup a little more than usual. I hope it's not so obvious to Zack that I put in more effort tonight.

"Sort of," I respond shyly. Boys weren't ever something Mom and I spoke about. Between her illness and general paranoia about people's intentions, I never wanted to add to her worry. It seems odd to talk to an adult about boys.

"Hmmm... Sort of cute? Doesn't sound that exciting. Now, a resounding yes to cute, that I'd be interested in."

Her sarcasm breaks the awkwardness that I feel discussing boys with her. At least a little. She looks so sincere. I sit down on one of the stools, across the counter that separates the kitchen from the living room.

"He's cute. I meant that was sort of why I took a little time to get dressed. Is it that obvious? Did I overdo it?" Looking down, I examine my outfit for the hundredth time. I bite my lip pensively.

"It doesn't really matter if it is, his jaw will be hanging open when he sees you in that sundress." Aunt Claire replies warmly. "Do I know the boy? I know a lot of kids from the hospital, broken arms and all." She unloads another glass from the dishwasher and reaches up to place it on the top shelf.

"I don't know. His name is Zack Martin." I turn, seeing his classic car pull up in front of the house. "There he is now."

The glass Aunt Claire was reaching to put away slips from her hands, shattering all over the floor.

"Are you okay? Did you cut yourself?" I rush into the kitchen, sidestepping shards of glass as best I can.

"Uhmm....yes, yes. I'm fine. Just clumsy. Go. I don't want you cutting yourself in here. Go have fun." Her voice is a bit shaky, startled from the piercing sound of glass hitting the tile.

"Are you sure?"

"Yes. Have fun. Be home by midnight, please."

Zack is just starting up the walkway when I open the front door. He looks up and I watch his eyes take me in. Slowly. They rake over me, dropping from my eyes to my glossed lips down to my exposed shoulders. Taking his time, he follows the neckline of my simple, yet body contouring sundress, lingering when he reaches my full breasts. I'm sufficiently covered, but I'd be lying if I said I wasn't aware that the dress showed off my assets well. Tight around my chest, gathering snuggly at the waist, with a scant amount of cleavage. Just enough coverage to still leave something for him to imagine. And I watch his face change as his imagination takes off running.

His eyes drift down my legs, tanned now from the eternal California sun. Momentarily he's lost in what he sees and doesn't even notice I'm watching him leer. Totally worth the extra effort getting ready tonight, I couldn't be happier at the reaction I get.

Eventually, his eyes make their way back up to mine and I arch one eyebrow, letting him know he's been caught. A normal reaction might be to look embarrassed or perhaps even flustered a little. But not Zack. Instead, he flashes me a wicked grin. "You look incredible." He's the one doing the leering, yet I'm the one who ends up blushing.

Chapter 22

Zack

We arrive at Meson Ole before it gets crowded. Nobody goes to dinner in Long Beach at six o'clock, except old people. Nikki and I are directed to a quiet spot in the back corner that overlooks the outside dinner deck and ocean beyond it.

"Unless you want to sit outside?" the half interested waitress says as she points to the table in the corner.

One glance at Nikki longingly gazing out the window at the water and I say, "An outside table would be great if you could manage that."

I hold the deck door as Nikki walks out, my gentlemanly gesture rewarded by the first view of her from behind. Holy shit, this girl makes my pulse race more than running eight laps this afternoon did. And it completely throws me every time.

She's sexy as hell, but it isn't just her smokin' curves in that form-fitting little sundress. There's an honesty about her — something that makes her so real. In Kardashian California, everything is planned, performed and perfected. Except for Nikki.

"Zack? Are you going to just stand there holding the door or join me for dinner? I think the loser has to actually eat dinner with the winner, not just stare at her from afar."

Caught fantasizing about Nikki's ass, it's my turn to blush—something Nikki does a lot. From the amused look on her face, I'm quite sure she knows exactly where the blush is rising from too. I don't think for a second that she's oblivious to the effect she has on me. It would be nearly impossible to miss.

"Is it too warm for you to sit outside?" I ask as the waitress glides past, heading back inside to get us a bowl of chips and salsa.

"I think you're warmer than I am," Nikki teases.

As I stand behind her to pull out her chair, a slight breeze catches Nikki's sundress and exposes her upper thighs. Her petite hand catches it before it goes any higher and smoothes it under her as she quickly sits.

The table is small, intimate. Taking my seat across from her, I pick up the menu, hoping to distract myself from the pulsating sensation I feel everywhere. My leg brushes against her long smooth one under the table.

"What do you like best?" Nikki asks.

It takes me a few beats to realize we're talking about the menu. Good... let's stick to the menu. I can handle that.

"I haven't been here in years. But I used to like the steak fajitas. I was a kid though."

"I actually know a few adults who eat steak fajitas too."

Before I can respond, the waitress returns.

"We'll both have the steak fajitas...from the grown-up menu," Nikki beats me to the punch, a mischievous smile on her face.

I smile, sitting back to soak in the freshness of whatever is brewing between us. My shoulders relax as I mentally begin to accept what my body has already surrendered to. From the corner of my eye, I notice a pretty, albeit artificial-looking, blonde teen and her mother are seated a few tables away. The girl looks strikingly like Emily. Suddenly, whatever I'd begun to accept seems oh so wrong.

Why the hell did I think that I could be a normal guy flirting with a girl I'm attracted to? It always comes back to Emily. And it should. I'm being selfish, trying to change the inevitable.

As I shutter over the feelings I don't deserve to feel, the conversation falls quiet. Nikki notices the change. I see a look of confusion replace the sexy smile I was enjoying just moments ago.

I don't want to hurt her. She doesn't deserve the crazy ups and downs that I put anyone close to me through. At least Mom and Dad understand why I sometimes withdraw or lash out. They get it. It doesn't make it right, but at least they know it's about Emily, not them. Nikki could never understand. And if she did, she wouldn't want to be here with me in the first place.

Awkwardness sets in. "So," I say, "what do you think of California? You moved from Texas, right?"

Nikki squints, confused at how the warmth between us turned icy so quickly, although she seems relieved that I'm talking. Unlike a few of our past encounters that went sour, I don't run away at least.

"Yes, Texas," she says, without the energy that was in her voice moments ago.

"Why did your family decide to move?" I ask with genuine curiosity since I've spent a lot of time thinking about getting out of Long Beach since Emily died.

Nikki hesitates before answering. In her face, I see a look I know too well. Apprehension. Desolation. Pain. Whatever I said to put it there, I wish like hell I could take back. "My...family didn't move. I moved in with my Aunt Claire, who lives in Long Beach. My mom passed away last winter and I don't have anyone else."

I'm speechless once again around this girl, this time for a different reason. She lost her mother last winter when I lost Emily? Is that why she seems so different from everyone else? Does she understand silence?

Trying my best to regain my voice, I clear my throat as I reach across the table and take her hand. "I'm sorry, Nikki. I am so sorry, I— "

Perhaps uncomfortable with the rawness of the moment, Nikki smiles at me shyly, her voice cracking, "Thank you. I don't talk about it much. It's still hard." She shrugs, an attempt to make light of it, but she doesn't fool me.

I start to say that I understand. How much I truly understand what she's been through…what she's probably feeling. The loss we share may even be the tie that binds us. But before I get to utter a word, the air between us fills with oniony steam as the waitress slaps down our steaming steak fajitas. Instantly, I'm yanked back to reality, my brain taking over for my heart.

I don't tell Nikki that I understand. I don't tell her about my loss. About Emily. I don't tell her that I know what it feels like to have your life torn apart. Instead, I decide to make her feel happy. Even if it just lasts for tonight.

The rest of our dinner is exactly that— enjoyable. It's lighthearted and full of easy, playful teasing. It's what Nikki needs. Maybe a part of me even needs it too, because I haven't felt this comfortable with another person in a long time. I wonder if I've *ever* felt this comfortable with another person.

Normally, I'd be restless in a restaurant after more time than it takes to consume my meal, but she and I while away two hours talking. I fill her in on all things Long Beach High…track, football, teachers, classes. We laugh when I share infamous stories about Keller, and Nikki tells me about her best friend back in Texas. For at least a little while, we're just two teenagers having a great time, rather than battling our private demons.

As we leave the restaurant and head back to the car, I selfishly make sure that Nikki walks in front of me.

Chapter 23

Nikki

When the car door closes, the tension increases. Dinner was surprisingly light after my telling Zack about Mom. It was just what I needed. Zack seemed wounded by my news, yet he didn't dwell on it...he didn't try to get me to talk about my feelings. Instead we moved forward, without looking back. It was almost as if he understood that it was a loss that words couldn't explain.

But now, with our close proximity inside Zack's car, the tension is anything but light. There's a current in the air and I feel it from the tips of my toes to the top of my head. Zack rolls down the window and fidgets awkwardly. I wonder if he feels it too.

We drive in silence for a few minutes, until it becomes clear we're going in the opposite direction we should be heading. "I don't know the area well, but doesn't Keller live near school? Are we still meeting at his place?"

"I want to show you something." We make eye contact. Zack seems excited, if a bit sheepish. It's a good look for him, terribly attractive. "You said you'd never seen the Pacific Ocean. I thought you might enjoy this view." He motions out the window. From the hilly point where he's now pulled over, the ocean crashes below us.

He jogs around the car, opens my door and takes my hand to help me out. A knowing grin spreads across Zack's face when he spots the goose-bumps on my arms. "I have a sweatshirt in the back if you're cold." We both know my shiver has nothing to do with the temperature. I shake my head.

"High Pointe Landing," he says, coaxing me out, even though I don't really need any coaxing. "It's meant for cars to pull over, so it's safe to get out. Great spot to see the sun go down."

"It's beautiful." I'm mesmerized, although I'm not sure if it's from the breathtaking view in front of me or the fact that Zack still hasn't let go of my hand. "And you're right. I've never seen the Pacific before tonight I've never seen any ocean like this," I confess.

Closing my eyes, I take a deep breath, smelling the ocean salt in the air, then exhale loudly with a hum. "California really is a beautiful place. I never intended to like it, but it's close to impossible not to be blown away by the weather and the beauty."

Zack cocks his head. "You didn't intend to like it? Why not? You mean, because you love Texas so much?"

I try not to laugh, but I can't help it. The thought of loving the trailer where I lived better than this is just comical. "There's not a lot to love back in Texas, Zack. At least not any part I ever lived in."

"How many parts did you live in?" Zack appears sincerely curious.

"Oh, my mom and I moved a lot. Never very far but lots of different small towns in the middle of the state," I explain. It's more than I've told anyone about the life Mom and I lived— even Aunt Claire— but it feels natural and right to tell Zack.

"It must be kind of cool to get to know different places. I've always lived in the same house. Sometimes I wish we'd move. A new place. Seeing things for the first time. Sort of like starting over."

"I don't know about cool. My whole life, I've wished I could live in the same house for years on end. I always thought it would be fun to know your neighbors. Maybe have barbeques and share things. I've never had real neighbors like Aunt Claire does. She talks to them all the time. I bet your family does the same thing."

Zack turns from our conversation, leaving his back facing me. What the heck did I say this time? Every time I begin enjoying his company, he disappears on me. I'm starting to get familiar with what happens, I just don't get *why* it happens. But this time I feel braver and intend to find out.

I walk around, giving Zack no choice but to face me. I grab his hand, hoping to restore our connection...get a reaction of some sort at least. But he looks down at me blankly. "What happened? You were right here with me a minute ago and now you're gone. Did I say something? Do something?"

He shakes his head, mute.

"Okay. But whatever it was, I can't promise not to do it again if I don't even know what I keep doing that upsets you."

"You don't upset me." Zack brings his eyes back to mine, briefly, then looks away again. Whatever it is, it's causing him pain and I want it to go away. I just want the anguish I see in his eyes to disappear.

"It's okay. We don't have to talk about it." I look down at my watch. "It's probably time we head to meet the group anyway." I squeeze his hand and take a step toward the car, our hands still locked. He tightens his grip, but doesn't move with me. It stops me in my tracks.

"I had a girlfriend," he begins. His voice is low and he looks down as he speaks. He pauses and I wait anxiously for whatever is to come next.

"Her name was Emily." Zack lowers himself to the ground and sits on the tuft of grass in front of the car, staring out at the sun setting over an ocean that is bluer than I ever thought it could be.

Forgetting my anxiety about getting so close to Zack, I sit down next to him and wait, knowing that whatever he's about to share brings him only pain. I want to support him. Just be here for him.

Zack turns to me, and with just enough light left from the setting sun, I see a fullness in his eyes that only fighting back tears can bring. I'm surprised when he speaks. "She was my neighbor for ten years. She died in a car accident six months ago." And with those two short sentences, Zack has told me more about who he is than a lifetime of words could ever tell me.

I close my eyes, realizing the pain I must have caused when I told him all I ever wanted was a neighbor. Nothing I can say will comfort him...I should know that from experience. So I don't try to give him words filled with false hope that things will get better, because I'm not sure they will. Instead, I rise to my knees, crawl between his parted legs, wrap my arms around his neck and just hold him. No words. No promises. Just silence and whatever comfort my arms can bring. He's tense for a few minutes. But I stay steadfast, keeping myself wrapped tightly around him, even if he doesn't hold me back. Until eventually, his shoulders soften and I hear his muffled tears.

We stay that way until the sun sets behind the ocean and all the light fades away. A lighthouse flashes occasionally in the distance. After a while, Zack pulls back and finds my eyes. "I don't talk about it, Nikki," he whispers. "People are afraid to talk to me about it, so they just pretend it didn't happen. Allie tried to talk to me once, but I shut her out and she knew better than to try again. I don't want to shut you out. I feel like you understand me. I felt that way even before you told me about your mom."

I lean my head against his shoulder. A few minutes pass and the flicker of the guiding light off in the distance catches my attention again. "I've always been drawn to pictures of lighthouses," I say. "I never understood why." As if on cue, it flickers again, revealing itself for a few seconds before it fades back into the darkness. "There's just something solitary about them, but at the same time they draw people in…guide them…maybe even save a few, just by giving them light in the darkness." Zack exhales audibly and rests his head against mine.

We stay that way, in the darkness, in silence, the only sound the waves crashing against the shoreline below us. Only thirty minutes pass before we climb back into the car, but it feels like thirty days. We're close enough now, even in the car, that our bodies touch, but this time there isn't a sexual energy. It's different. Acceptance— and understanding. Around Zack, I feel…at home. Like I belong. Something I never thought I'd feel again.

Chapter 24

Zack

The minute the front door opens, I immediately catch on that Keller is wearing a clean shirt and has dosed himself with cologne. My mind darts back to the football field conversation. Keller plans on asking Nikki to the homecoming dance. *Shit.*

"Hey. Oh, you came together. Okay, great." Keller raises an eyebrow to me as he lets us in.

"Zack lost a bet and had to buy me dinner," Nikki says more to tease me than in response to Keller.

"You must have bet Zack that I'd kick his ass in football yesterday," Keller grabs a Coke from the fridge.

"No, we had a bet as to whether you were actually human. I bet you were, because I was dying to take Nikki to dinner."

Keller comes at me from behind, grabbing me into a headlock. Lifting his feet, his weight easily brings me to the ground. He hops on top of me like a cat pouncing on a bird. His goofy grin is full the entire time.

"See, he's not human," I shove him off of me and climb to my feet to rejoin Nikki.

"Well it's about time you got here, now get your asses in the den and do some work. You think it's a coincidence I joined your group?" Keller hoots as we move into the den. "I don't actually like you. I just know you'll do the damn work and I can ride on your A."

"An A? Well if you average that with 4 Ds and 2 Fs, you're looking at a solid D this semester. I bet that report card makes the refrigerator!" Keller and I have been busting each other's balls since we met in peewee football. It's pretty much a requirement to torture a guy when you spend a few hours a day leaning over his ass waiting for the ball to snap.

"Keller is a lot smarter than he wants us all to know," Allie says climbing off the couch to greet us.

"How dare you, Allie. We're supposed to be friends and now you're trying to ruin my reputation," Keller teases. "I'm going to slip a hunk of beef jerky into your vegan smegan bean salad."

Allie laughs. "Have you ever tried black bean burgers, Nikki?" She knows she's not getting anywhere with the rest of us in her quest to convert us all to vegans.

"Uhm, Nikki just ate steak fajitas, Allie. I tried to get her to eat bean curd fajitas but she insisted on the juicy, tender steak. I had no choice but to join her." I drop onto the couch, pulling Nikki with me.

"To be honest, Allie, until you, I'd never even met a vegan—or a vegetarian, for that matter. The only thing bigger than a Texas hat is a Texas steak. The bigger the better, is the motto."

"Oh, Nikki, Nikki, Nikki..." Keller jumps to attention. "The bigger the better is a California motto too." He wiggles his eyebrows suggestively. Nobody laughs louder than Keller laughing at himself.

Nikki's blush reminds me what a contradiction she is. She can tease with the best of them, but there isn't a crude bone in her body. And I look over to remind myself what a beautiful body it is.

Busted. Nikki catches my eye and raises a brow. But she clearly isn't disturbed that I was looking. She's smiling and...she seems happy. Something changed on that hill tonight. There's an unspoken bond between us. It's always been there, we just hadn't acknowledged it existed.

Oblivious to the way Nikki and I are consumed with each other, Allie continues her rant. "I hope they have vegetarian dishes at the homecoming dance this year. Last year I nearly fainted from hunger. I don't know how in 2014 there can be a school menu without vegetarian entrees. It's barbaric"

"Speaking of dances," Keller jumps to his feet. For a guy who must weigh 250, he hopped to attention pretty damn fast.

"No, Keller, no. We aren't speaking of dances. We are working on an English Project." I draw out the words. "Remember?"

Keller, to my surprise, actually gets the hint. But I should have known better than to challenge him with Nikki nearby.

"Looks like somebody changed his mind since yesterday. Decide you're taking someone to the dance?" he taunts, just as the doorbell pings. From the corner of my eye, I catch Allie's head flying up. Her gaze bounces between me and Nikki. "Saved By The Bell, Zack. Get it, Zack? Get it?" Keller flounders through his own fit of desperate laughter as he opens the door for Cory, the last member of our group.

I'm not sure if she was doing it on purpose, but Nikki kept me distracted most of the night. Sitting next to me on the couch while we argued over what to include in our project, her bare knee brushed up against mine more than once. Each time I looked up at her, she smiled innocently.

It's after eleven when we finally wrap it up. "Can you give me a ride, Zack?" Allie asks, hesitating slightly. "My car is still in the shop."

"Sure. Cory?"

"I'm good. Took my brother's car. Hopefully he didn't wake up." Cory smiles.

We say goodnight and Keller walks us to the door.

I open the front door to the Charger and Allie and Nikki look at each other. Allie seems to make a decision, giving me her unspoken blessing. "Go ahead, I get out first anyway," she says to Nikki, then gives me a wink, both of us certain Nikki has no idea that dropping off Allie first is actually completely out of the way.

We pull up in front of Nikki's and I turn off the engine.

"You coming in with me?" Nikki teases.

"If you invite me." I nudge closer to her.

"I...I..." I know she's turning pink, even though it's dark out and I can't see her color.

"I was just teasing."

"Oh."

"Listen, about the dance."

"Yes?" she asks, her voice perking up a bit.

"I don't want to go."

"Oh." Deflated, she responds.

"But I don't want you to go either," I say as a means of clarifying my earlier statement. But it only confuses things more.

"I don't understand?"

"Keller was going to ask you to go to the dance tonight."

"He was?"

"Yeah...couldn't you tell? He had on a shirt without stains and didn't smell too bad," I say.

She laughs. Then we fall into awkward silence. I turn, pulling my knee up on the seat to face her. There's just enough moonlight to see her face. "Listen. I didn't want Keller to ask you to the dance, because I wanted to be the one to go with you."

"Okay…" she trails off, waiting for me to explain.

"But I don't want to go to the dance."

"But you don't want me to go with Keller either?"

"No, I definitely don't want you going with anyone else." I rake my fingers through my hair, certain I'm bungling this. Then a thought dawns on me. But it makes more sense in my head than when I say it aloud. "Nikki, would you *not* go to the dance with me?"

She laughs. "And what does *not* going to the dance entail, exactly?"

"I don't know. We'll go somewhere. Just not to the dance."

She laughs and shakes her head. "Sure. I'd love to *not* go to the dance with you, Zack."

"Perfect." Out of the corner of my eye, I catch the blinds on the front windows of the house move. Nikki turns, following my line of sight. The blinds move again. "I think we're being watched," I nod toward the house.

Nikki gasps. "Oh my god, we so are. I can't believe my Aunt Claire is a snoop."

I grin. "She's probably just worried about you."

"I guess."

"But she's totally aunt-blocking the kiss I've been thinking about for hours."

Nikki whirls back around. "You've been thinking about kissing me for hours?"

Shit. I didn't mean to give that much away. "Ever since you intentionally brushed your leg up against mine," I say.

"I did not *intentionally* brush my leg against yours!" Nikki protests. I was teasing, but her denying it so vehemently, makes me wonder if maybe she really did.

"And the way you moved your mouth while you were reading…"

"What about the way I moved my mouth?" Defensively, Nikki questions.

"You know."

"No, I don't know."

Scooting closer to her on the old bench seat, I wrap my hand around her neck and pull her close. Her sharp intake of breath is audible. "Then you better get inside if you don't want your Aunt to see me kiss you."

This close, we're both breathing heavily. I only mean to tease her, but I'm finding it hard to keep my resolve with her body so close to mine. She's dangerous.

"Go!" I growl, afraid I'll change my mind and give her aunt a good show. With a last, lingering look, she gets out of the car. I know I should probably walk her to the door. But I'm not sure I can even walk, so instead I wait till she's safely inside before I pull away.

Nikki

I lay on my back in the center of my bed, turning and turning the small hospital bands between my fingers. In the few weeks that I've been here, I've taken them out faithfully every night. Every night except for the last two nights since Zack and I sat along the overlook.

I don't know how Zack and I found each other, but it's the first time in my life that I'm starting to wonder if there really is such a thing as fate. Before now, fate was an escape...a fantasy, something that only happened in movies and books, where people paid for a happily ever after. Now I wonder if maybe, just maybe, I wound up here for a reason. Finding Zack— learning that he's as wounded, lost and in need of a connection as I am— somehow validates I'm on the right path to wherever it is I'm going.

I've had boyfriends before. Well, sort of. I've kissed two and even let one get to second base. I say "let" because it just seemed like something I should experience...a hurdle I needed to cross before hitting a certain age I guess.

But how I feel with Zack is different. Really different. I *want* what's happening to happen as much as he does. So much so that

I've even let the search for my sister take a back seat to spending time with him. As I look down at the bracelets in my hand, I feel guilty for letting anything cloud my focus.

Aunt Claire knocks on my closed door. I shove the bracelets under the pillow and sit up just before she walks in.

"So, you haven't changed your mind about missing the homecoming dance tonight?"

"No." I shake my head. The morning after Zack asked me out, I was excited to tell Aunt Claire. Unfortunately, the feeling didn't seem to be a shared one. Ashley thinks I'm overanalyzing it, that Aunt Claire is just concerned with me dating any boy. After all, this is new to her too. It's just that she seemed excited when I told her someone asked me out, but deflated so quickly when I mentioned it was Zack. At first, I thought maybe she knew him, knew what he'd been through, but when I asked, she said she'd never met him before. Yet I've had the odd feeling her concern is more about *who* my date is, rather than about my going on a date at all.

"What are you two going to do tonight on your non-dance date?" Aunt Claire asks, sidestepping my boxes to sit on the edge of my bed. She hasn't asked why I haven't unpacked yet, it makes me wonder if she understands.

"I don't know." I shrug. "We haven't really talked about it. Get something to eat, I guess. Maybe go down to the beach."

Aunt Claire's mouth opens, then closes. Then opens. "Oh," is all she says. Although I'm certain there is more she wants to add.

"Is everything okay?" I ask.

She forces a smile. "I'm just nervous about you going on a date."

"I'm almost eighteen."

"I know, I know. It's not that I don't think you're old enough. It's just..." Her voice trails off and she pauses for a moment. "I'm not sure what advice to give you."

"Don't worry, Ash already gave me advice," I tease, trying to make her feel better.

"Do I even want to know what advice she gave you?" Aunt Claire has met Ashley and knows she's a bit on the crazy side.

"She told me not to get in a car with anyone drinking, and to order the most expensive thing on the menu." And to always use a condom, but I leave that part off.

She smiles, and this time it's genuine. "That's actually good advice."

"Ash wouldn't steer me wrong," I say playfully, bumping shoulders with her.

"I'm working a double at the hospital, so I'm not home till tomorrow morning. But that doesn't change curfew."

"I know."

"Okay." She stands. "Have fun." She walks toward the door and looks back before stepping through. "But not too much fun."

I realize I may have gotten ready a tad bit too early. Almost a full hour is left before Zack is supposed to pick me up and my nerves are already getting the best of me. The ice maker in the freezer makes a loud clank as it drops freshly made ice into the holding bin, and it scares the heck out of me. I actually jump at the sound, even though I've heard it dozens of times since I've been here.

With too much time on my hands, I rethink my outfit. I blow through a dozen outfits, everything from shorts and a tank top to a pretty, although a bit too fancy, sundress. Finally I settle on a simple black skirt that's short, but not too short, and has a flirty, fun bounce to it. I pair it with a plain pale pink t-shirt with girly capped sleeves, and sandals...part of the American Apparel shopping spree that Aunt Claire and I went on when I first moved in. Checking out my reflection in the mirror, I find a California girl staring back at me, rather than a Texan.

Even though I had time to waste, I'm barely finished brushing my teeth when Zack's car pulls up outside. The rumble of his classic Charger immediately sets fluttering whatever butterflies had settled over the last hour. My heart stammers a million miles a minute as I reach for the doorknob, so much so that I have to force a deep breath in and out to stop myself from passing out. Remembering how Mom always calmed herself when she was nervous or panicky, I close my eyes and count silently. *Ten, nine, eight, seven, six*...on one, I finally open the door.

The minute my eyes land on him, the gentle butterflies in my stomach turn into a violent swarm of bees. For a second, I really think I might vomit. Zack squints. "Hey. You okay?" He steps toward me, his face full of concern. The close proximity only makes my momentary panic worse. I nod.

"You sure? You look kind of pale." The corner of his mouth twitches. "Even for you."

"Yes," I snap out of my daze. "I think the heat just caught up to me today," I lie.

Zack smiles, a cocky, confident smile. "I get that a lot. The room gets warmer when I walk in."

I roll my eyes. "You're full of yourself today."

He hands me a folded up piece of paper and walks past me, heading straight to the kitchen. Making himself at home, he opens a few cabinet doors until he finds a glass. I unfold the note and smile as I read it. *You look beautiful.* Zack glances over at me, arches an eyebrow and smiles.

"Drink." He orders, handing me a full glass of cold water. My brows furrow together, I've forgotten my own lie. "You said the heat was getting to you," he reminds me. "Drink."

I sip the water, but I'm really not thirsty. "Where are we going?"

"Not to the dance."

"I got that much the other night."

"Finish your water and I'll show you."

It's the start of my favorite time of day, the hour before dusk, when the sun's heat settles down but still shines brightly. Zack pulls onto the Pacific Coast Highway and reaches for the dashboard to turn on the air conditioning.

"Would you mind if we rolled down the windows instead?" I ask. It's beautiful out. Eighty in southern California, without the humidity, is very different than eighty in Texas.

"Really?" He cuts his eyes to me, checking to see if I'm serious, then quickly returns them to the road.

I nod.

Grinning, he pushes the button on his window and I do the same. "Figured you'd be all worried about your hair."

I shrug. "You're the one who has to look at me."

He doesn't respond, but his smile says it all. We kid around about our lack of talking, but I really am able to tell a lot about him without any words. I know he has three different smiles. One that's a polite gesture, but really doesn't mean he's happy. One that he forces when he's trying to cover up for how he really feels. And then there's my favorite. The one that makes it all the way up to his eyes. Dimples dip deep, his blue eyes sparkle and it's absolutely contagious. I can't help but smile back when I see that one.

"What kind of music do you like?" He pushes buttons on the dashboard. The radio begins to play.

"Anything. I don't really have a set type. It depends on my mood I guess."

Zack glances over to me, our eyes catching for a split second before his return to the road. "What kind of mood are you in now?"

I debate the question internally for a moment. "A singing one, so that means pop."

His eyes stay on the road, but I can see smile number three in his profile. There's a slight squint in the corner of his eyes and the caverns of his dimples warm me. "Can you sing?"

"I can."

He glances at me suspiciously, then back to the road. "I mean, can you sing *well?*"

"Nope. But I don't let that stop me."

He shakes his head. "By all means, go right ahead."

"Oh. I don't do solos."

"You don't do solos?" he repeats, a chuckle in his voice.

"Nope. I usually have a different duet partner, but you'll do."

"I'll do, huh?" His smile fades momentarily. "Who's your usual duet partner?"

"My best friend, Ashley, back in Texas."

His smile returns. "So you don't have a duet partner here in California?"

"Nope…I was thinking of asking Keller…" I trail off, acting coy.

Zack glances at me, assessing the seriousness of my words. "Cute. Find a rock song. I don't do pop performances."

The half an hour drive to wherever it is we're going might just be the most fun I've had since Ashley and I were down at the lake last. Not surprisingly, Zack can actually carry a tune— his singing is pretty damn good, especially compared to mine. We pull off the road and drive a few blocks, slowing as we enter a driveway into a park.

"We're going to the park?"

"Sort of."

A few more minutes of driving into the heavily wooded park and we come upon a clearing. A huge lighthouse comes into view in the near distance.

"Is that the lighthouse from the other night?" I ask excitedly.

"Yep." Zack says, looking satisfied with my reaction.

It's beautiful. I'm not sure if I'm more in awe of the breathtaking structure sitting perched on the edge of land before us, or the boy that remembered what I'd said the other night. I think back to our conversation, about how I'd always been drawn to lighthouses as I watched this one flicker off in the distance. The fact that he remembered something so insignificant during our emotionally intense conversation, tells me a lot about who he is.

We drive farther down the road and I'm surprised the parking lot next to the lighthouse is empty. The sun is just beginning to set and I can only imagine how much more incredible the colorful sky in the backdrop will get. "How come no one is here?"

Zack shrugs. "I guess people take it for granted, forget it's even here."

He turns off the engine and comes around to open my door, offering me his hand. The boys back in Texas that I hung out with definitely don't have manners like Zack.

He doesn't release my hand, and when he helps me out, we're standing a few feet apart, facing each other. My pulse accelerates when he takes a step closer to me. He places one hand on the car behind me and with the other gently smoothes my hair.

"Your hair's a mess," he says quietly. His words are teasing but his eyes roam my face with an intensity that tells me he isn't really thinking about my hair.

His hand drops to my cheek, his thumb stroking softly as he moves in even closer. We're toe to toe, our bodies not actually touching, yet I feel the electricity radiating from his to mine. "You're different than other girls."

137

Left Behind

That's good, I think? I don't respond, because I'm not sure he expects me to answer and I have no idea what to say anyway.

"Nikki?" He leans down ever so slightly, but he's close enough so I feel his breath on my neck. I can't look up, I'm afraid if I do, I might melt. And it has nothing to do with the heat...not from the sun anyway.

"Nikki?" He calls my name again, this time more forcefully. My eyes jump to meet his. He's so right there, it scares the hell out of me, but I don't dare turn away. His eyes drop to my lips. "I haven't been able to think about anything but kissing you for days." His voice is low and throaty. I'm amazed that I'm still standing and haven't dropped to the floor in a puddle.

"All I can think about is your lips. The way they move, the way each syllable forms a different shape and sometimes I see a hint of your tongue flash and it makes me crazy. I want to feel your lips against mine so badly it hurts."

Closing the distance between us, Zack uses his body to guide mine up against the car. I feel every part of his hard body pressed firmly into mine. *Every* part. His hand at my cheek drops to my neck and his thumb grazes my collarbone. My skin breaks out in goose-bumps when his gentle hold tightens to a grip. A devilish grin teases at his lips— he likes the reaction his touch elicits from me. His strong hand wraps around my neck and he squeezes gently, forcing my head upwards to meet his stare.

Just as his head begins to drop down, his mouth parting to meet mine, a car pulls up next to us. Directly next to us, in a parking lot full of empty spots. A man's voice smacks me back into reality.

"Park closes at nightfall," the ranger says pointedly.

Zack groans before he takes a step back and turns around, giving the officer his attention. "Yes, sir. I was just going to show my girlfriend the lighthouse. She's from Texas and has never seen one up close."

138

The ranger looks between me and Zack, eyeing us suspiciously, then nods. "Okay. You two have a good night then. Just mind the closing time, son."

Zack nods and the Ranger drives away. The entire exchange is less than one minute, but it effectively kills the moment. His expression a cross between deflated and amused, Zack growls and takes my hand. "Ranger-blocked," he mumbles as he leads me toward the lighthouse. For the next few minutes, he rambles on about the history of the lighthouse and something about ships that used to dock in the area, but my brain is still stuck on two simple words he said. *My girlfriend.*

Deep orange and vivid shades of purple and pink fill the sky as the golden sun makes its way down past the edge of the ocean. With only the sparkling deep blue sea as the backdrop while the sun sets, it looks as if the endless Pacific is swallowing the shining orb. We watch in silence as it disappears right before our eyes. The waves crashing the rock jetty below us leaves a mist of salt water in the air.

"I guess we better go. The ranger will probably be coming back to check on us and it's almost dark," I say, hating to even bring it up as we sit on the outside deck at the top of the lighthouse. Our shoulders pressed against each other as we watch the sunset keeps me warm, even though the air has chilled with the disappearance of the sun.

Without a word, Zack stands, offering me his hand. My back against the wall of the lighthouse, he places one hand on either side of my head, caging me in. His eyes sparkling in what little remains of the daylight, he smiles widely as he slowly shakes his head.

"No?" I whisper, his nearness clouding my brain and making me forget what he is even responding to.

He shakes his head again. Leaning in slowly, he whispers in my ear, "No way I'm going anywhere until I kiss you. And up here, I'm thinking there's a lot less chance of being interrupted again." God, the sound of his throaty voice, his warm breath on my sensitive skin, and the thought of his lips finally touching mine— it's almost too much.

He draws his head back, his eyes meeting mine, and I find the need I'm feeling throughout my body reflected back at me. My breaths become shallow and closer together, and the muscles in my thighs tighten as I watch his eyes drop to my lips and then rise to meet my gaze again. And then ever so slowly, he leans in and kisses me. At first it's gentle, almost hesitant. But that doesn't last long. I lean into him, my pert nipples push up against his hard chest and a sound that can only best be described as a growl comes from deep within him.

Our kiss deepens, becoming hungrier, more forceful. He wraps his hand around my neck, guiding my head to the position that he wants me. I cling to him, my hands grasping at his shirt, wanting more, *needing* it more than wanting it. We seem to have a rhythm together, our tongues dancing with familiarity even though they've only just met.

Dusk has fallen into night by the time we both break away, breathless. I take a deep breath, trying to regain my wits, but it's no use. Zack's eyes smolder as he runs his knuckles along my cheek and looks into my eyes. His breath is labored and it makes me feel good that he's as affected as I am. He doesn't say a word; instead, he smiles, a real, full-mouth smile, his sexy, deep dimples telling me more than words can say. Again, without words, this boy has taken my breath away, and maybe even a little piece of my heart.

Time seems to fly by the rest of the night. The kiss relieved some of the tension that's been weighing him down, because Zack's lighter, happier. I've seen bits and pieces of this side of him, in small glimpses, but it's never lasted very long. Until tonight. We laugh through dinner and fight over music as he drives me home.

"Wonder if we'll have an audience soon," Zack says as he turns off the engine in front of Aunt Claire's house.

"Not tonight. My Aunt is working the overnight shift at the hospital."

Grinning widely, Zack pulls me across the bench seat onto his lap. I yelp in surprise, but there's no place else I'd rather be.

"So that means I can kiss you as long as I want tonight?" He says with a devilish smile on his face. His hand, casually wrapped around my bare leg, caresses the outside of my thigh. I wonder if he has any idea what the simple stroke of his fingers on my skin does to me. It sets my body on fire and turns my brain to mush.

"I'm supposed to be home at midnight," I whisper, wishing it wasn't true.

Zack kisses my lips once, his mouth still lightly pressed against mine as he speaks, so I can feel each syllable as I hear it. "You are home."

"I guess I am." I smile. "She did say I had to be home. She wasn't specific about being inside." I wrap my hands around his neck.

The corners of Zack's mouth curl up. "Now you're talking."

I don't look at the time when I finally leave the car, but the windows are completely fogged. We both groan a bit and I can tell that it won't be long before our kisses become something more. We can't keep our hands off of each other. The things he makes me feel scare the hell out of me, but excite me even more.

Zack insists on walking me to the door this time. He kisses me a few more times, and then hands me a folded-up paper before he walks away with just a smile. Leaning up against the inside of the door, I wait to open the note until I can no longer hear the rumble of his car as he pulls away. *I had a great time tonight* is scribbled on the piece of paper. The smile is still on my face when I fall asleep an hour later.

I wake to Aunt Claire knocking gently on my door. When I don't answer, she opens the door ever so slightly to check if I'm inside. As I hear the door open I notice Zack's note half on my pillow and half stuck to my cheek by sleep drool. How attractive.

I quickly fold the note and stuff it under my pillow as I see Aunt Claire's eyes peer in through the cracked door. "Wanted to check on you. I just got home." Obviously she's worried about how far my date went last night.

"How was your date with Zack?" she asks as she slides her head in just a little bit farther. I feel bad about making her beg for information, so I sit up and welcome her into my space. She truly has been great about giving me privacy and a beautiful bedroom. She hasn't even complained about my boxes. I never had anything as special and private in my life and I worry that I haven't thanked her enough.

"Come in. You don't have to stand in the hall," I say with a smile.

Still in her hospital whites, Aunt Claire sits on my bed. She never had children of her own and she's still trying to figure out her role in our newfound relationship.

"So, did you have a nice not-go-to-the-dance date?"

I know I'm beaming, the flush of my cheeks telling more than my words. "It was really great." I stop short without saying anything else, suddenly remembering sitting on Zack's lap in the Charger long beyond midnight. She's a really cool Aunt, but I'm not too sure that would be cool with her.

"Great? Well, that's great, I guess."

I sense the disappointment my limited response evokes, but I also think I spot some concern in her voice. I want to assure her everything is fine. More than fine actually.

"It was a great date, Aunt Claire." I tell her how Zack surprised me by taking me to a lighthouse because I'd mentioned I had never seen one up close before. Sounds harmless enough, right? Thank goodness she doesn't know that, minutes ago, I was dreaming about the feeling of Zack's hard body against mine as we shared our first kiss at the lighthouse.

Feeling like I should give her a little more, but not yet ready to reveal the change in my and Zack's relationship, I let her in on my idea.

"Zack runs too," I say. "He's actually really fast. I was thinking about running by his house to pick him up for a run this morning." I don't tell her it was actually Ash's idea during our 1 a.m. phone call where she pried for details of how far I went with Zack in the Charger.

Concern wrinkles her face. Does she think it's a bad idea? Is she just worried I'm moving too fast? "It's a hot day, Nikki. I'm not sure a run in this kind of heat is safe."

"The heat here is so much more bearable than in Texas!" I'm out of bed and grabbing clean running shorts from one of my boxes. "You can't even imagine the difference. I've run miles in way hotter weather than this. My body is used to it." I pause, and then add, "I think nursing makes you a perpetual worrier, Aunt Claire. I guess it's a hazard of the job," I smile attempting to lighten the suddenly serious mood. "

Aunt Claire, still holding onto a look of fear and concern, only says, "Go slow, Nikki."

143

Chapter 26

Zack

"Zack? Zack, honey, you have company. Can you come down, please?" Mom sounds nervous.

I have company? The only person who ever comes by anymore is Keller and Keller hasn't seen ten on a Sunday once in the twelve years I've known him.

I throw on a t-shirt and grab my Dodgers hat. A few steps down the stairs, I hear Mom mid conversation with another woman. I thought she said the company was for me?

From the top of the stairs, I catch a glimpse of a ponytail. Her back is to the steps, but I'd know that laugh anywhere...and the image of that ass is permanently scorched into my brain. Nikki is in my house, talking to Mom.

The creak of my footsteps on the wooden stairs alerts Nikki to my presence and she turns before I hit the landing. "Hi Zack," she says, with energy that usually only comes from a bag of Swedish fish chased by a Red Bull. I spot her nervous smile as she speaks.

"I was out for a run and thought you might want to join me. It's beautiful out," she talks fast.

Mom is smiling even broader than Nikki. She looks like the sun just came out after a thunderstorm. I didn't realize how long it's been since I saw Mom light up with real happiness. I savor the moment.

"You want to race me again? I *let* you win last time. Don't think I'm doing it twice," I say with a grin.

She turns to my mom, her face full of innocence. "Zack didn't let me win, Mrs. Martin. He's trying to rewrite history to cope with the fact that he was beaten by a girl." She turns to me. "Did you get a good night's sleep?" Nikki arches an eyebrow and attempts to conceal her smirk. "You sure you're up for a rematch? I don't want you to have any excuses when I beat you again."

After the hours in the car last night, she knows I didn't get a good night sleep. I look to see if Mom picks up on her flirting. It's a side of Nikki I've only seen just a glimpse of before, but I like it. A lot. It does something to me when she's bold, pushing past her limit even though it scares her.

Mom doesn't catch the meaning of our exchange since she doesn't know about our date last night. I'm sure she assumed I was out with Keller— he's the only person I've been out with anywhere since Emily. But Mom is obviously pleased with Nikki's light-hearted and happy way because she beams from ear to ear.

"A rematch? You sure you know what you're asking for?" I catch her eye and her cheeks immediately turn a glowing pink. I love that I can do that to her with only eye contact and some words with hidden meaning.

"I'm sure. Unless you're scared to go up against me again?"

"I'll change into running clothes," I say. I take the stairs two at a time to change into shorts and sneakers.

Nikki's laughter wafts up the stairs as I change. Mom's follows it. Damn, it's a good sound.

When I come back downstairs Mom is humming to a Billy Joel song softly playing on the kitchen satellite radio as she's pureeing veggies in her juicer. "She's stretching on the front porch. I like her, Zack." Mom's face is full of hope.

"Me too, Mom. Me too."

A tear pools in Mom's eye. "Aw, don't, Mom… just don't. Guys don't do the happy tears thing. Please."

She nods and waves me off with a laugh. "You're impossible. Go for your run. Have a great time. You deserve to have fun. You really do, sweetheart."

"Hope you didn't pull anything stretching." Earbuds in, Nikki doesn't hear me come out. She's surprised at my appearance, her thoughts obviously off somewhere else. I hope she's stuck in the same place I've been for the last nine hours.

"Zack, who is that man?" She's staring across the street at Mr. Bennett, who's working in his flowerbed.

I hesitate. "It's Mr. Bennett…Emily's father. He spends a lot of time gardening since Emily…"

Nikki's hand reaches out to touch my arm. "I'm sorry. I didn't know. I didn't mean to make you uncomfortable. He just looks so familiar to me."

I look over in Mr. Bennett's direction, where Nikki's eyes are fixed. A male voice calls out from the house, "Dad, phone for you. It's the hospital. I think you need to take it." Mr. Bennett sets down his spade and strips his hands of gloves before heading back to the house.

Nikki turns to me. "Is someone in the hospital?"

"No. Mr. Bennett works at Long Beach University Hospital. He's a psychiatrist."

"Really? That's where Aunt Claire works. I wonder if they know each other. Is it a big place?"

"Biggest in Long Beach." I shrug.

"The guy calling him Dad… Emily has a brother? Does he go to our school?"

I clear my throat to ease the knot that's caught there. I suppose it's only normal for Nikki to be curious, but the conversation makes me uncomfortable nonetheless. "Yes, Brent. He comes home to visit every few weeks now. He never did that before. He's older than us— I think he was fifteen or sixteen already when Emily was born. The Bennetts were already in their forties when Emily came along. I don't know him very well. He lives in New York. A writer, I think."

Before she can ask another question, I start down the driveway. "I'll give you a head start. Come on."

"Head start?" she says, insulted at the notion. "I don't need a head start. I'm faster than you think, Zack. Don't underestimate me." She blows by me, sprinting down the street.

"I'd never underestimate you, Nikki," I call as I breeze past her with a grin.

Nearly two miles later, with Nikki not far behind me, I direct our run into Dover Park. Mom used to take me for long walks in my stroller here. It still makes me feel like a kid, running through the trails.

When we get into the center of the path, I slow down and head to the bench area alongside the flower gardens. There's a water fountain between the benches and Nikki reaches me just as I'm splashing water on my face.

"You only stopped because you knew I was going to pass you. Admit it," Nikki taunts, flat out of breath from our little sprint.

"You're breathing a little heavy. That always happens when women run behind me," I tease.

She finishes her drink from the fountain and turns to me with a cocked eyebrow. "I seem to remember it's you who likes the view when I'm in the front."

Well, she's not wrong there. The sight is goddamn spectacular. Why didn't I slow down and let her pass me? My competiveness just cost me ten minutes of heaven's view.

"Aunt Claire asked me to go brunch with some friends of hers from college." Nikki glances around as we settle down on a bench under a large, shade-bearing oak tree. "She worries that she doesn't spend enough time with me because of her long hours at the hospital."

"It's nice that she cares so much. I can't imagine how hard it is to lose a parent, but at least you had an Aunt that you were close to and weren't alone."

Nikki looks off into the distance. "To be honest, I didn't even know I had an aunt until Mom died. They didn't speak. My mom…meant well, but she kept a lot of secrets. She always thought she was protecting me. She was very sick." Shadows from the past cloud her face.

But today I want only sunshine. "Not everyone would bounce back so quickly. You're strong," I say, lightly bumping her shoulder with mine and resisting the urge to add my own confessions. I jump to my feet. "But not strong enough to beat me. First one back to my house has to make the loser a fruit smoothie."

I shoot past Nikki, but push my competitiveness aside after a minute in favor of the great view all the way home.

I throw a towel from the kitchen cabinet at Nikki. Not that her dripping sweat bothers me at all. In fact, there's nothing I'd rather do at the moment than trace the beads of perspiration sliding behind her tank top between her heaving cleavage.

"Thanks, I'm ready for my smoothie," she proudly orders not realizing the real prize was letting her stay ten feet ahead of me for two miles.

"Do you like cantaloupe?" I ask, digging through the fruit shelf in our refrigerator. "Mom is a fruit smoothie junkie, so if you prefer something else, I'm sure we have it." I toss a cantaloupe to Nikki.

She catches it and examines it. "Never had one."

I'm surprised, but she's not joking. I've only just started to scratch the surface of Nikki's past. Fresh fruit and family picnics probably weren't the norm.

"Then cantaloupe and melon smoothies it is. They're my specialty anyway."

Nikki watches me with a smile on her face as I slice the fruit. I think a guy making her something in the kitchen is a first.

"Here, taste," I move closer to feed her a piece of fresh sliced cantaloupe from my hand. My eyes are glued to her lips as she bites. A drop of cantaloupe juice glistens on the corner of her mouth and I use my tongue to wipe it off. Jesus, I just can't help myself around this girl.

A soft sigh slips from her lips when I move my mouth to her warm neck, my hard-on quickly growing against her stomach as I lean in. My entire body ignites when I feel her tremble from my kiss. The memory of that tremble woke me up more than once last night.

"Zack, what if your mom comes in?" she asks, breathless, as my kisses move further up her neck.

"She won't. She's out at the Farmer's Market," I whisper into her ear. Another shudder runs through her body. "Eleven. Every Sunday," I breathe. "Thankfully, she never misses it."

Trying my hardest to slow things down, afraid I'll scare her by pressing her up against the kitchen wall, which is only about two seconds away from happening, I lean back. "You taste like cantaloupe," I say. "I can't help it...I really, really, like cantaloupe."

150

Nikki laughs. "Guess I do too now."

I finish making our smoothies and the cool drink helps to turn down the heat in the kitchen. A little, at least. Trying to get the last bit out of the deep glass, Nikki spills the remainder of hers onto her tank top.

"God, I'm a klutz." She laughs, totally unselfconsciously.

"I can give you a t-shirt if you want." I grin. "In fact, I think I really like the idea of you in my t-shirt."

Nikki blushes as our eyes meet.

"Come on up and pick one." I start up the stairs so she doesn't have time to consider not following.

Upstairs in my room, I pull open my drawer to reveal dozens of impeccably pressed and folded t-shirts. My mother definitely has issues.

"Wow, it looks like someone dumped a whole table from Abercrombie," Nikki arches her right eyebrow towards my t-shirt drawer.

"Cute. You too, huh? Keller likes to take pictures and post them on Instagram to try and embarrass me. His drawers are the polar opposite. Crap sticking out all over the place. I found a half-eaten cheeseburger in one of his drawers last year." Even a two-minute stay in my room turns to twenty minutes of him busting my balls over how neat it is. "My mother is an organization freak."

"I'm afraid to touch one and disturb the artful presentation," Nikki teases.

I grab the smallest t-shirt I can find, hoping it will be tight in all the right places, and toss it at her.

"Great, thanks." She turns.

"Leaving with my shirt?" I ask.

"I was just going to look for the bathroom to change." The pink sting is back in her cheeks as she awkwardly tries to figure out if I really expected her to undress in the middle of my room.

151

As much as I'd love to watch her take off her shirt, and the pink in her cheeks certainly stirs something inside me, I let her off the hook. Kissing her chastely on the lips, I say, "Change right here. I'm going to take a quick shower anyway. I have a feeling you're being polite and not mentioning what I smell like."

"I did make you sweat pretty hard," she smiles.

I know she means the race but I walk over to her and say, "Yes, you really make me sweat." She laughs and pushes me towards the door.

Five minutes later I find Nikki in my room with that old t-shirt of mine on. It's as tight as I expected, a perfect fit for my liking.

"I borrowed your brush too. Tried to do something with this mess of hair," She runs her fingers through her now loose, shiny hair.

"It's beautiful," I say as I reach her space and quickly invade it.

She's backed against my desk chair and only feet from my bed. The trouble alarm is going off at a blaring volume in my head. But the need to touch her again, feel her body against mine like it was last night, outweighs any concern about where things might lead to. My thumb brushes her parted lips and my body responds instantly when she lets out a low gasp with a sharp intake of breath. Screw it— concern about where things might lead quickly turns to hope that they will. Just as I lean in, Nikki dodges my kiss and turns to my desk. Nervously, aiming to lighten the moment, she lifts something, dangling it from her finger with a cheeky grin. "Aren't we a little old for a Batman mask, Zack?"

Her hands are on the mask Emily gave me on my 12th birthday, our little private joke. The life drains out of my body as I snatch it from her hands.

I take two steps back. Two steps away from her physically, but miles of distance stretches between us suddenly.

"You should probably go," I say, walking to the door of my room. The look on Nikki's face causes me physical pain. She's confused. Hurt. Probably even a little embarrassed. Selfishly, I wallow in the feel of my own pain as it washes over me, ignoring the sadness etched into her face as I escort her to the front door.

Chapter 27

Nikki

I stand at the top of Zack's driveway, staring blankly ahead. For a second, I feel like I might have imagined the last five minutes. Then I turn back and see the closed front door, the sound of it slamming shut behind me ringing in my memory over and over again. *What the hell just happened?* I half expect him to open the door and tell me he's joking.

But he doesn't.

Feeling tears well in my eyes, I blink, trying to dam the flood looming just beneath the surface. *I can't cry. Not here.* I squeeze my eyes shut and ball my fists until my nails dig deep enough into my palms that it causes me pain. Taking a deep breath, I dig my iPod from my pocket, spin the volume up as high as it can go and pop in both earbuds.

Concentrating only on forcing one foot in front of the other, I make it down the long driveway just as tears begin to blur my vision. I'm about to turn from the house and take off running, when a hand grabs me.

Whipping around, I rip the earbud from my ear as the woman repeats the words she's just said. Only this time I can hear them. "Your name?"

"What?" Confused, I ask, even though I've heard her question. She doesn't repeat herself. Instead she just stares at me. I look down at my arm, where she's holding me just below the elbow. Her hold is strong and suddenly I feel nervous even though it's the middle of the day and we're out in the wide open.

Her face is hard and serious, as if I'm trying her patience, even though she's the one with her hands on me. I attempt to pull my arm from her grip, but it's no use, her fingers are locked around me.

"Nikki," I say.

She keeps her eyes locked on me but releases my arm. I should run, but something keeps me standing in place. "Why are you here?"

It's a question I'm not sure I know the answer to. What the hell *am* I doing here? Zack didn't invite me. I just showed up. The tears I'd been fighting win out and trickle down my cheeks. "I don't know. But I shouldn't have come."

The woman makes no move to follow me as I take off running. She just stands there, motionless, staring in my direction as I run away.

By the time Aunt Claire comes to my room to tell me we're leaving for brunch soon, I'm not lying when I tell her I'm sick. I drowned the sound of my sobs in a shower long enough for my skin to prune and turn bright red. My head throbs with the aftermath of my crying jag.

"I hope it's not the flu," she says, feeling my head for the second time. "The ER has been pummeled by the flu this year. I don't know why people don't take their kids for shots." Realizing my mom probably hadn't thought about the flu, she backtracks. "I'm sorry, Nikki, I didn't mean…."

"It's fine, Aunt Claire. I know what you meant. And I'm sure it's not the flu."

She looks at her watch and then back to me. "Maybe I should stay home."

"To watch me sleep? No, you go. You've been looking forward to seeing your friends. I'll be fine. I promise."

She looks torn, but agrees. "You'll call me if you feel any worse?"

"Yes."

"You promise?"

"I promise." I smile, feeling comforted by her concern and wanting to reassure her.

Exhausted from my own emotions running a marathon, I fall asleep for a while. I wake up to my phone chiming. A glimmer of hope fills my heart. It could be Zack apologizing. Maybe he was just having a bad day and realized how much he hurt me.

I swallow back tears at seeing Allie's name on my phone. Not ready to give up hope, I scroll down just in case I've missed a text. There's nothing from Zack. Allie wants to go to a movie. She's become a good friend, but I'm not in the mood. I text back that I'm not feeling well. But all I really want is to talk to Ashley.

I dial Ashley's cell, silently praying that her mother has paid the bill. She answers on the second ring and I roll onto my side in the fetal position, ready to spill my guts.

"Hey," I say. "You busy?"

"Not at all. Supposed to be watching my Mother's four spawn but a rerun of Jackass is on, so the TV is babysitting."

"Even the six year old?"

"It's Jackass, every age loves it."

I laugh. "I wasn't worried he wouldn't love it. Just wondering if a six year old should be watching it."

"I'd read to them," she says defensively. "But I don't have any books now that you're gone." I hear the squeak of the rusty-hinged front door open and then slam shut. She's gone outside to talk. "How are you?"

"I've been better." I sigh, rolling onto my back.

"What happened? Whose ass do I need to kick?"

I feel pathetic and sad and a whole lot confused. "I don't know." A tear slowly rolls down my face. "I have no idea."

"Start from the beginning," Ashley says. And I do. I tell her about the lighthouse and the kiss and how great everything was. How thoughtful Zack seemed and all of the time we spent steaming up the car windows. Even as I tell her, the whole day makes no sense. I suppose I thought walking through the last few weeks aloud would bring an ah-ha moment. Where everything would finally click and make sense. But it only confuses me more.

"So he basically leaned in to kiss you and then walked you out."

"Basically." It sounds ridiculous to say it, but it's really how I see things happened.

"Maybe he's got the crazies like your Mom."

"Bipolar," I correct her for the millionth time.

"Whatever. He sounds like he's got it. Maybe you're a carrier and you gave it to him when you kissed him." She's teasing, trying to make me feel better.

"Oh and I didn't tell you the weird part," I say.

"You mean there's a part that's weirder than him groping you then showing you the door?"

"The weird part isn't about Zack. It's about the woman."

"What woman?"

"The one that was staring at me on the first day of school. Remember? I told you about her. It sort of freaked me out for a minute. But then she just disappeared."

"Okay."

"She grabbed me when I was leaving Zack's house and started questioning me."

"Questioning you about what?"

"Why I was at Zack's house, I guess."

"What did she say?"

"She asked me my name and then asked what I was doing there." I picture the woman's face as I speak. She was angry."

"Who is she?"

"I have no idea. But her and Zack both definitely didn't want me there."

"I wish I was there with you. I'd go kick Zack's ass for you."

"Only Zack's ass? What about the woman?"

"I'd kick her ass using Zack's limp body as a battering ram."

I smile, because she definitely would.

We talk for a while longer and I feel a little better when I hang up. At least I'm starting to feel less like it's something I did.

I need to clear my brain of Zack and trying to figure out what happened. Aunt Claire won't be home for hours, so I decide to take the time to look around in the attic. I've snooped through most of the house already, the attic is my last hope to find something about my sister. Aunt Claire showed me the staircase when I first moved in but told me that there was nothing to see but boxes and things in storage. Although she and I have made a lot of progress becoming more comfortable with each other, we still don't talk openly about my mom or my life before Mom died. It's always very shallow. I just wish we could both lay our cards on the table. I'm tired of playing solitaire.

The attic is neat and organized. No surprise there. Aunt Claire keeps her life very orderly. Exactly the opposite of how Mom was. There are a lot of boxes. Most are labeled with things like, "Nursing school text books" or "Size 6 winter clothing". In the corner behind a bunch of other boxes I find one labeled, "Childhood photos and papers."

Unlike all the other boxes it isn't taped closed. It looks like Aunt Claire has been in this box recently. Maybe when she learned Mom died she went back and looked at old memories.

Even though I feel increasingly guilty for violating Aunt Claire's trust with each snooping session, I decide to look inside. She never put any restrictions on where I went in the house or what I touched. Never said I couldn't look at anything. I keep trying to convince myself I'm not doing something wrong, but I know better.

The box is full of loose papers and pictures. It isn't neat and organized like the rest of Aunt Claire's life. There are dozens of school pictures of Aunt Claire. Her and Mom looked a lot alike when they were young.

I find stacks of old report cards— lots of As, perfect attendance and glowing praise from teachers. I wonder what Mom's say. I can't imagine they had the same comments. Mom was definitely much more of a rebel than Aunt Claire— that's one thing I know.

At the bottom of the box I find a large manila envelope labeled "Hospital Records". Maybe it's about Aunt Claire's husband. She doesn't talk about him very much, but she told me he had cancer and was very sick. I know he was in the hospital for a long time before he died.

I open the envelope, finding yellowed pages. Aunt Claire's husband only died five years ago. As I flip through the papers, a knot in my stomach forms finding a set of baby footprints. The kind the hospital gives a mom when her baby is born. It's labeled "Baby Girl A."

I don't know if the footprints are mine or my sister's. I trace the outline of the tiny feet with my finger. The feet are as small as a doll's, they don't seem big enough to belong to a real baby. I hadn't thought about whether we were born full term or not. The miniature footprints make me think we must have been born premature.

Behind the footprints is a document titled "Discharge Note." I read it slowly learning more than I thought any box would reveal.

Baby Girl A was very sick. She was in the hospital for two months before she was allowed to go home. The note talks about surgery and procedures and things I don't really understand. I consider asking Allie if she would ask her dad about the procedures since he's an obstetrician. But I haven't told Allie anything about my family and I'm not sure I'm ready to let anyone but Ash in on my secrets.

Nothing in the records identifies my sister. Mostly it's a pile of medical jargon I don't understand. All of it documenting just one baby— Baby Girl A.

The sound of a car pulling into the driveway seizes me with panic. A peek out the curtained window finds Aunt Claire, her car door already opened. *Shit*. I've been up here for more hours than I realized. I hastily drop the papers back into the box and close it, shoving it back into the corner. I dart downstairs, hop into bed, and pretend I'm sleeping when Aunt Claire cracks the door open to check on me.

Nikki

I don't hear from Zack the rest of the weekend. By Monday morning I'm a combustible mix of anger and hurt that I think might explode by the time I get to see his face in sixth period English. But I never get the chance. Instead, I stare at his empty seat for forty-six minutes, anxiously waiting for him to walk in.

By Tuesday, my nerves are on edge with worry. This time, he shows up to class, although it might have been easier if he didn't. My heart speeds up at the sight of him, and I actually feel relief that he's okay. There are two empty seats in the room. The seat he's been sitting in every day, directly in front of me, and one on the opposite end of the room. Our eyes lock when he enters just before the bell rings. Then he walks to the other side of the room and sits down. He never looks back, not even when he walks out the door at the end of class.

A week later it's become abundantly clear that he no longer even wants to be friends. He's going to just continue to ignore me and pretend nothing ever happened. And I guess I'll do the same. But it's easier said than done. Unlike him, what I felt was real.

Concern and worry turn to anger. I've replayed the whole morning we last spent together a million times in my head. I'm convinced I did nothing wrong. Yet I can't help but wonder what set him off. There's something that flips a switch inside of him that makes him retreat. Like a ticking time bomb, only I have no idea what will make it go off.

I've lived a life of not knowing what I was walking into each day. The last week has had me thinking a lot about Mom and her disease. The highs and the lows, and the lack of anything in the middle. Mental illness is easier to accept than someone that just decides they're done with you.

"There's a party tomorrow night at Keller's house," Allie says, as the bell rings signaling the end of lunch. "His parents are going out of town and next week is his eighteenth birthday." I already knew because Keller had told me about it every day this week. "I'll pick you up at seven."

"I don't know, Allie. I wasn't really planning on going."

"I know. That's why I'm picking you up. So you can't tell me you're going to go and then not show up."

"But…" I try to think of an excuse of why I can't go, other than the obvious one.

"Seven," she warns and walks away leaving me no time to argue.

It's six o'clock on Saturday evening and I'm getting ready to go to a party I really don't want to go to. Aside from the fact that I'm in a mood Aunt Claire dubs melancholy, there's a good chance Zack will be there since Keller is one of his best friends.

I ignore the bell when it rings, because it's too early for it to be Allie. But a few minutes later Aunt Claire knocks on the door and let's Allie into my room.

"Hey. I'm sorry, I thought you were coming at seven."

"I was, but I thought I'd come early." She plops on my bed and looks around the room. Her brows furrow at all my packed, neatly organized boxes, yet she doesn't ask any questions.

"Well, I can be ready fast. I don't take that long."

"No rush. I thought maybe you'd want to talk."

I look at her questioningly and she raises her eyebrows in response. We both know what she's talking about. It's been the ten ton elephant in the room for the last two weeks. Allie's a smart girl. Observant. No doubt she's watched me stare at Zack's back during English class, tears threatening at my eyes almost daily.

"Is it that obvious?" I sigh, feeling relieved to talk about it with someone other than Ashley. Don't get me wrong, Ash is awesome, but she doesn't know Zack, so I can't really get her perspective on things. Other than her Zack bashing from hearing a one sided story.

"That you two are both miserable? Yeah, it's pretty obvious." She smiles.

"I think you're mistaking indifference for miserable on Zack's part."

"Nope, I'm pretty sure he's miserable."

"Why would *he* be miserable? He's the one who stopped speaking to me."

"I don't know, Nikki. But I see the way he looks at you. He's crazy about you."

"Well, he has a funny way of showing it."

"I know, I wish I knew what was going on in that head of his. But I know he cares about you. I think he's just still struggling to accept Emily's death."

165

"My mom died around the same time as Emily. I struggle too. Some days are better than others. But I don't take it out on people I care about."

"My Dad is an obstetrician at the hospital where Emily's Dad works. I asked him how her Dad was after the accident and he said he didn't talk about it at all. People handle things in different ways."

"I guess." I finish braiding my hair to the side and brush on a little mascara.

"Let's go have a good time," Allie says. "Forget Zack. I like him…I really do. But it's his loss."

I hear the music blaring from Keller's house before we even turn the corner to his street. His green, impeccably manicured front lawn is littered with seniors…and red cups. We have to park almost a half block away, because the street is lined with car after car.

The front porch is filled with guys I don't know, but recognize from the football team. I've watched them practice as I ran the track, most of my attention focused on a certain quarterback, but the others still look vaguely familiar. Keller stumbles out the front door just as we approach. He must have started the partying a little before the party started.

"My two favorite ladies have arrived!" He chugs back the contents of his red Solo cup, tosses it over his shoulder and lunges at me and Allie. Taking each of us in an arm, he lifts us off the ground at the knees and carries us to the door as if we are feather light.

"Boys." He calls the attention of the three large guys sitting at a table on the porch arguing over a game with cups and a ball. They turn and smile broadly. "Who's got the bowl?" Keller gently sets us down.

A guy stands and extends a large glass fishbowl in our direction filled with keys. Allie shakes her head no.

"You in?" he asks me.

"Oh, I'm not driving," I say, assuming he's collecting the keys of drivers to ward off potential drinking and driving.

Key Collector smiles at me. He's cute, in an oversized bear kind of way. He leans down, a wry grin on his face, and whispers in my ear. "It's a key party. You put your keys in to decide who you're hooking up with later."

OH! "No thanks," I feel the pink spread across my cheeks.

"That's too bad. I'd love to pull your key." He winks and walks away.

"Come on," Allie yells over the music and grabs my hand, leading me away. I look back and find key party guy watching me and smiling.

Inside, the music is even louder. I feel the bass thumping in the hollow of my chest and my heart speeds up to pump with the rhythm. There are people everywhere, some I recognize, others look a few years older. People sway to the music, a few couples are already splattered around the room in corners making out and groping each other.

There's a card game going on in the kitchen and I think it might be strip poker since two boys are shirtless and one girl is looking worried and taking off her socks.

"What do you want to drink?" Allie yells over the music as we weave through the crowd toward the makeshift bar set up on the dining room table. I smile when I see the green bottle that reminds me of one of the few times I'd gotten drunk back in Texas with Ashley.

"Nothing for me. Thanks."

"Are you sure?" I knew Allie was planning on drinking, we'd already talked about us walking home. It's a nice night and I like to walk anyway.

"Yeah, I'm good."

An hour into the party and I finally start to relax when there's no sign of Zack. Drunks can be quite amusing to talk with when you're sober. Allie and I settle in at a table in the yard where Keller is holding court, telling joke after joke. Sometimes he screws up the punch line, but those times he's even funnier. One of the guys from the football team delivers a new, full cup and Keller knocks the entire thing back in one ridiculously large gulp.

Almost knocking the entire patio table over as he pushes himself away from the table, Keller stands and reaches his arms over his back, pulling his shirt off in one tug. Such a boy way to undress.

"Time for a swim," he says with a mischievous smile on his face that makes me nervous. "What do you think, Nikki, you want to go for a swim?" He lifts me out my chair and into his arms, completely ignoring my protests.

"Oh my god, Keller. No!" I scream as he makes his way to the side of the large, rectangular in-ground pool.

He swings me back and forth as if he's going to toss me in. "1, 2…3!" On three he swings me higher but doesn't really let go. My heart pounds in my chest.

"Please, Keller. I can't swim!" I lie, screeching my words.

"That's okay, I've got you." He grins and makes his way around to the low diving board. Standing at the edge, he jumps up and down with me still in his arms. After the second jump, he wobbles on the landing.

"Keller, please! You're going to fall in." I cling to his neck. With each bounce he loses his grip on me a little bit more.

Another bounce, followed by a barely salvaged landing, and I hear *his* voice.

"Put her down Keller," Zack bellows, his tone clipped. I crane my neck behind Keller's wide girth to see Zack standing at the edge of the pool.

Keller turns, looking to Zack and then me. He deliberates on his choices, then mumbles a few words before carrying me back to the patio. He sets me down next to Zack and walks away with a salute.

Zack looks at me for a long moment, "You okay?"

I nod.

He nods back, then walks away without looking back.

So maybe my solution to the discomfort I feel knowing Zack is around isn't the smartest one. Reluctantly, I take the shot I'm offered and swallow it back. It burns going down and the effect is immediate. Although the instant effect may have more to do with the five beers I drank in the hour before the shots started flying.

The cute guy with the nice smile who was collecting keys on the porch refills my glass with a clear liquid. It looks innocent enough. Me, Allie and Key Collector clank our shots together in cheers. Half of mine spills all over the counter as I bumble just to keep the tiny glass in my unsteady hand.

"Come on," he pleads with his playful smile. "You girls have to give me your keys. You're the two hottest girls here."

Allie finally gives in, tossing her keys in the bowl. I manage to ignore their pressuring me to join them, excusing my drunk self to find the ladies' room. In my intoxicated state it takes me a good ten minutes to do what should take three.

Opening the bathroom door, I turn down the dark hallway and stop in my tracks when I see Zack. A girl I recognize from school is all over him. We lock eyes, but he makes no attempt to speak to me.

Stumbling back into the kitchen, I find Allie and Key Collector where I left them. The crushing sensation in my chest hurts so much that I can barely breathe. I reach into my pocket and pull out my house keys and dangle them in the air.

"Yes!" Key Collector yells victoriously, pumping his fist in the air for added effect.

A few minutes later, smiling widely, Key Collector announces it's time to distribute the keys. Allie and I dance together and my body begins to feel the music. Really feel the music. Relaxed, inebriated, I sway to the rhythm, finally forgetting what I'd started drinking to forget. Mission accomplished.

My eyes falling closed, I almost miss Zack stalking over to me. Keller follows in his wake, looking harried.

"Wasn't my idea, man," Keller holds his hands up as if to plead his innocence.

"Let's go," Growling, Zack says to me.

"No," I respond adamantly. I don't have to listen to him. Keller's standing behind Zack, his eyes go wide.

"You're leaving. If I have to carry you out of here, I will."

Swaying a bit as I try my damnedest to stand still, I fold my arms over my chest and call his bluff. Zack looks to Keller. "Walk Allie home later."

"You got it," Keller replies quickly, looking to Allie, who nods back.

I don't even bother to protest when Zack scoops me off my feet and into his arms. Suddenly, I'm too tired to argue. Leaning my head against his chest, I breathe in deep and close my eyes at the soapy smell that makes me relax. I don't even open my eyes to see Key Collector still holding his bloody nose when we pass him sitting on the front porch.

"What time does your Aunt come home in the morning?" Zack asks as he tucks me into my bed. I must have slept the entire time since leaving Keller's living room.

"Eight," I mumble.

He slips into bed next to me and hauls me close to him, wrapping his arms around my waist tightly.

"I missed you," he whispers as he buries his head in my neck.

"I'm mad at you," I whisper back.

"I know," he answers.

"But I missed you too," I admit, my voice fading as I fall asleep feeling more at peace than I have in two weeks.

I crack one eye open, the brightness in the room causing pain in my eye that can only be matched by the throbbing in my head. I groan. The events of last night come flooding back and I reach behind me only to find a cold, empty bed. *Was I dreaming he was lying in bed with me?* I turn around to look, but the room is empty— he's gone. There's a folded up piece of paper on the nightstand, along with two pills and a bottle of water.

I unfold the note; the crinkling of the paper is deafening even though it's barely audible. *I'm sorry. Take the Tylenol. Drink the full bottle of water, you need to hydrate. Pick you up at 8pm.*

Chapter 29

Zack

They say there are five stages of grief. I don't even remember what a few of them are, but it felt like I was stuck in anger and depression for a very long time. People tried to explain it to me, help me through the process, but I wouldn't take any of the hands that were offered. Guilt and shame barricaded me alone on one side, feeling disconnected from the rest of the world on the other.

I'm scared of waking up one day and *not* thinking about Emily. I blamed Nikki for consuming my thoughts...for taking up space that I thought should belong to Emily. But maybe there's room for both of them.

It's the first time I've come to visit Emily without being angry. I didn't come to say goodbye or tell her I've moved on...because I'm pretty sure I'll never fully be free. But instead I'm here to tell her I finally found a place for her. One I will cherish forever and keep with me willingly instead of fighting where she's always belonged.

Placing the bunch of lilacs I brought at her grave, I take a few minutes to think back to all the good times we shared. The good memories, not the bad.

Wiping my sweaty palms on my jeans, I take a deep breath and walk to Nikki's door. I have no idea what to expect. For two weeks I was a total asshole to her, pretending she didn't exist. Then last night I storm off with her in my arms like some caveman. Hell, I'd be pissed at me.

Seeing her at the party, how vulnerable she was from too much alcohol, how much hurt was in her eyes when she saw me — I knew I needed to fix what I'd broken. I'd made the choice to walk away from someone I cared about once, and it's something I'll regret every day for the rest of my life.

My own feelings aren't important. I can live with the sadness that has wrapped around my heart and squeezed so hard I can barely breathe. Hell, I've *wanted* the pain ever since I lost Emily. But I can't hurt Nikki anymore. And I definitely can't let her *get* hurt. I'm crazy about this girl. Maybe, just maybe, fate brought us together for a reason. To fix each other, not obliterate our already wounded hearts.

I just hope I can convince her to trust me yet again.

I ring the bell and wait. She answers but doesn't immediately invite me in. Pulling out the big bouquet of flowers I've hidden behind my back, I offer them and a folded note as I do my best puppy-dog-eyed beg for forgiveness.

She tries to hide it, but there's a smile tempting her lips. She rolls her eyes, shakes her head, then steps aside for me to enter.

"How are you feeling?" I ask.

"Do you mean the hangover or the wounded heart?" she asks jokingly, but I see in her face she's not entirely kidding. Busying herself with putting the flowers in water, she avoids eye contact. I take the vase she's filling from her hands and dump the flowers in unceremoniously, just to get her attention.

Her back is to the kitchen counter and she doesn't move when I step to her, invading her personal space. I cup her cheeks and wait till she looks up. "I meant the hangover, but I'd like to hear about the wounded heart too," I say quietly.

"Well, the Tylenol and water took the edge off the hangover. My stomach is still queasy, but I think I'll live."

My thumb caresses her cheek. "And your heart?" I lean in. My own is beating like thunder in my chest, I'm pretty sure she must be able to feel it too.

"It's…," she struggles for a word. "Confused."

"Your heart's confused or your head?"

She thinks about it for a moment. "My head, I guess."

"So your heart isn't confused?" Lowering my head to meet with hers, I speak directly into her eyes.

She shakes her head.

"Good. I'm glad. Mine isn't either."

"But I don't understand what happened." Her eyes perk up with hope, then turn wary again. "One minute everything was great and the next minute you couldn't stand the sight of me."

I fucking hate that I made her feel that way. Seeing the pain in her face, hearing it in her voice, causes a physical ache inside my gut. Like I took a punch and it's all I can do to not double over from the pain.

I swallow hard. I need to make her believe what she means to me. So I tell her the truth, even though sharing the memory will hurt both of us. "The first time I met Emily, I was nine years old and standing in the street in Batman briefs. It became her nickname for me. Emily bought me the batman mask you found in my room for my twelfth birthday." I'm quiet for a long moment, trying to come up with the right words. I take her hand, lacing our fingers together and wait until she looks into my eyes before I begin. Then I tell her the truth, let the words flow from my heart, even though they scare me to confess them.

"I could never not stand the sight of you. Hell, Nikki, when you walk into a room, I see you in color when everything else is

175

black and white. I'm just screwed up. I feel like it's wrong for me to be happy. I don't deserve it. So I try to make myself feel something different."

Her face looks sad. "I feel like that sometimes, too. Like I shouldn't be smiling so soon after my mom is gone. I feel guilty when I'm enjoying school. When I'm laughing with Aunt Claire. Sometimes even when I feel good around you."

"How do you deal with it?"

She shrugs and forces a weak smile. "I focus on things that give me hope." Behind her words, there's so much pain. But she works at pushing past it. Something I need to start to do.

"I didn't have hope until I met you." I stare at her. She's stunningly beautiful, and not just on the outside. Her full lips speak healing words. Her big blue eyes seek the sun, even on a cloudy day. She searches my face, trying to see if I'm being honest, I don't blame her for being cautious.

"I'm afraid, Zack. You hurt me. You made me doubt myself. My own judgment."

"I'm sorry. I'm so sorry. I know I hurt you. But please give me another chance. I can't promise you I'll never screw up again. But I can promise you that I'll try. I'll try every day." I pause, gently lifting her chin to force her gaze back to mine. "I'm crazy about you. Every time I see you smile, knowing I put it there, it makes me happy. *You* make me happy. I don't want to fight it anymore."

The corners of her mouth tilt upward, she wants to accept what I'm telling her, but still looks conflicted. "Your head is telling you to throw my ass out the door, but your heart is telling you something different, isn't it?"

A real smile lights up her face. "Yep." It's contagious; my own smile surfaces for the first time in weeks.

I wrap my arms around her waist and pull her close. "Which one's louder?"

She furrows her brow.

"Your head or your heart. Which one is yelling at you louder?"

She looks down, then back up, our eyes locking. "My heart."

"Go with your heart. Let me prove to your head that your heart made the right choice."

She bites her lip. "You'll talk to me when you're struggling? Not shut me out?"

"I will," I say without hesitation.

"You'll never shut me out without explanation again?"

"I won't."

Her eyes search mine a final time. "Fine." She breathes out.

"You'll give me another chance?" I ask, filled with hope.

"Yes. But you're on probation."

"Got it. Probation." I tighten my hold around her waist, bringing her flush against me.

"I'll support you however I can, but you need to work on *you*."

"I will."

"You better," she glares at me and warns.

"But…can I start working on me tomorrow?"

Her eyes squint and brows draw down.

"Tonight I'd rather work on you." I kiss her lips. "I want to show you how sorry I am."

We alternate between kissing and talking for hours, it's difficult to keep things from going further. But tonight is about moving forward. Together. Slowly. So I force myself to regain control every time I start to slip. It's not easy.

Hours later, Nikki's stomach growls as we lie side by side on the couch, her lips swollen from makeup kisses. "Hungry?" I chuckle.

She smiles. "A little."

"What did you eat today?"

"The Tylenol you left."

I draw my head back to see her full face. "You didn't eat anything at all?"

She shakes her head. "I was too queasy."

I slide out from alongside Nikki and lift off the couch. "Well let's fix that. What's Aunt Claire got in the fridge?" I head to the kitchen.

"Mostly healthy stuff," she says without much enthusiasm.

"Are you sure Allie and your Aunt Claire aren't related?" I yell with my head buried in the refrigerator. "You've got the same fake food in here that she eats."

"Aunt Claire doesn't even drink real milk. Almond or Soy." Nikki comes up behind me and scrunches her nose.

"What time is it?"

She checks her cell on the counter. "Eleven thirty." Something on her phone captures her attention.

"Everything okay?" I ask.

"Yeah. Just a few dozen texts from Ashley and some missed calls."

"Something happen?"

"I don't think so." She scrolls through her messages. "I told her you were coming over and she just wants to check on me."

I frown thinking of the conversation the two of them must have had with how I acted the last few weeks. "Sorry. She must be worried about you. Call her. Better Burger is open till midnight. I'll get us some burgers and give you some time to talk to her." I kiss her forehead before grabbing my keys.

"You sure?"

"Positive. What do you want?"

"Whatever. I'm easy."

I arch my eyebrows and grin. Kissing her chastely on the lips, I walk out leaving my girl with a flush face.

Nikki

I slide down the wall to sit alongside the front door, listening to the hum of Zack's Charger as it pulls away from the curb and sets out for Better Burger. My head is swirling, reliving each of the moments on the couch as I reach down to my jeans and pull out the note Zack handed me when he walked in. I forgot I'd even stuffed it in my pocket until now. My heart is racing as I open it. This little ritual with Zack has become something I so look forward to.

> *Nikki,*
>
> *You make my heart pound with excitement.*
>
> *My body tremble from your every touch.*
>
> *My mind long for your every word.*
>
> *I'm crazy about you.*
>
> *Please forgive me.*
>
> *Zack.*

I pinch myself because I'm sure it can't be real. He can't be real. I came to Long Beach to find a sister I never knew existed and I met a guy I'm crazy about. He's not perfect. Heck, neither am I. We both have a ton of emotional baggage. But I feel the bond to him down deep in my soul. Fate had to bring us together.

Forcing myself from my Zack-induced fog, I pick up the phone to call Ashley. It buzzes as my finger hovers over the keypad. *Ashley*. Who else would it be?

"You've got great timing, Ash," I say as I force myself to snap back from dreamland.

"I've heard that before. It's just one of the few amazing things about your best friend. There are so many others." Ashley laughs at herself.

"How are you?" she continues. "Did note guy re-break your heart over the last few hours? Because if he did, I'll be putting out my thumb and hitching a ride with the next creepy trucker that passes on by this crappy little town. See what a good friend I am? I'm willing to risk being murdered by creepy trucker guy just to come kick mutant note boy's ass if he hurt you again."

She has a unique way of saying it, but her point is sincere. Ashley means it. She'd walk to California if she thought I needed her. "Just the opposite, Ash. Everything is great. We talked, he apologized and explained why he has been struggling and things are good. I feel like we've made a lot of progress. He's here now. Well, not at the moment. He went out to get us burgers but he's coming back soon. I've never felt like this with a guy before, Ash. Never. I can't explain it."

"Oh, no. You're scaring me. This guy screwed with your head. Please don't say you're falling in love, Nikki. Love is dangerous and you're not ready for it. You're barely ready for a silly crush."

Her words hurt me, make me defensive. "Like you're so ready for it, Ash? Give me a break. You were in love four times last year and I put up with all of it. And this is different. So, so different. *It's real.* Whether you believe me or not." My tone lets Ashley know I don't want her to tease right now.

"Cool down. I believe you. I'm just worried about you. This guy has been snapping your heart back and forth since you got there. I don't trust him. That's all." I know Ashley means well but there's no way to explain what's going on between me and Zack. Our bond isn't something I can put into words, so I wouldn't expect her to understand.

"He's going to be back any minute, Ash. Can I call you later?" I feel badly blowing her off, I don't want to insult her, but I feel good for the first time in weeks, and I don't want her to bring my head down.

The doorbell rings as I'm standing in my room smoothing my hair back in place. "Burgers, fries, and chocolate shakes." Zack holds up two bulging paper bags when I open the door. "Aunt Claire would ban me if she knew. Actually, she'd probably ban me even if I were bringing in organic, free range tofu, if she knew what I was thinking about her niece."

"What were you thinking about me?" It's obvious from his tone, but I want to hear him say it.

Zack drops the bag on the table and pulls me into his arms. His eyes drop to my lips. "You want me to tell you?" he dares.

"Do I?" I ask coyly.

With a devilish smile on his face, Zack nods his head.

I swallow. "Tell me." My voice is barely a whisper.

"I was thinking about what you taste like. The way you feel underneath me. The little sound you make when you start to come undone."

I'm not sure if he hears it, but a barely audible whimper escapes my throat.

He kisses me. "Your Aunt Claire doesn't come home until eight o'clock in the morning tomorrow, right?"

I nod my head. Unconsciously, I lick my lips.

Zack growls. He steps back and shakes his head. "Go. Eat. I'm going to throw some cold water on my face." He heads toward the bathroom, mumbling. "Eat fast."

I lie in bed still awake as the sun rises, replaying the whole night with Zack in my head. I don't know how I'm supposed to fall sleep. A vision of Zack lying next to me in my bed, propped up on his elbow, flashes in my head.

"Are you a virgin?" He'd asked casually, while lightly drawing circles with his finger around my exposed belly button.

"Yes." His finger stopped tracing its path momentarily. "Does that bother you?" I asked, curious at his sudden halt.

He didn't respond verbally. Just shook his head slowly with a smile.

"So why did you hesitate?"

"I was taking a moment to thank God," he responded with a wicked grin.

I'm not used to talking to boys about sex. Or anyone for that matter. Mostly because there was never anything to talk about. So it took me a few minutes to muster the courage to ask.

"Are you?" I almost felt stupid asking. He'd had a long term relationship with Emily and....well, look at him. A lot of girls throw themselves at a guy like Zack.

I was shocked when he nodded his head. "I know it's hard to believe, since what girl could keep their hands off all my hotness, but yes, I am. And, I have to say, I actually don't mind at all right now. I'm glad that we both are. If we decide we're ready, it will make it that much more special." I almost melted.

It's not just our talking about sex and fooling around that keeps me awake, though. Although we did enough of both to keep my mind occupied for the entire day. Something bigger happened between us last night. More than an apology and an acceptance, we took a giant step forward. Agreeing to be open and honest, not hide the things that make us who we are. We connected in a way I've never felt with anyone before.

That's why I feel guilty. I didn't tell him about my sister. I wanted to. I really did. But the timing just never seemed right. I made him promise to be open and honest with me from now on, yet I'm still hiding my own secrets.

Nikki

onday afternoon at school, Zack meets me at my locker before English class. The hallway is beginning to clear out as kids duck into classrooms before the bell rings. Two doors down from our room, Zack tugs my hand and pulls me toward the emergency exit, leading me under the staircase.

"What are you doing?" I giggle as he pushes me up against the wall.

"I'm getting you alone. This place needs more spots for privacy."

"It's a school, Zack. I don't think they factored the necessity of places for privacy in when they built in."

"Well that's a shame." He steps toward me, leaning one arm on either side of my head against the wall.

"We're going to be late."

"I don't care. I haven't been able to stop thinking about your mouth since I left last night." His eyes drop to my lips. The bell rings but neither one of us attempts to move.

"My mouth?" I whisper, repeating his word on a pant, not really questioning.

A wicked grin on his face, he nods and moves closer. Our noses are almost touching. He lifts one hand and his thumb brushes my bottom lip. "These lips taunt me. Every time I close my eyes I picture them." I suck in a breath. "I need to kiss you now. I wouldn't have been able to wait two more periods until after school." His mouth crashes down on mine and he kisses me. Really kisses me. I get so lost while he completely ravishes my mouth, I don't even notice my books drop to the floor from my hands.

"Wow," I say, breathless, when we finally break for air.

He leans his forehead against mine. "Tell me about it. I'll be sitting in English class with a hard-on now." I blush, but totally love what our kiss can do to him.

"Nice of you to join us today, Mr. Martin, Ms. Fallon," Mr. Davis says as we walk into class five minutes late, my lips still swollen from our kiss. "Your lateness just volunteered one of you to be the first to share your poetry assignment with the class. Which one of you will it be?"

Zack looks to me; his eyes bulge for a second and he looks down then back to me. I follow where his eyes silently lead and find a noticeable swell in his pants. My eyes widen. Zack looks amused as he catches my gaze again.

"I'll do it, Mr. Davis," I volunteer. Zack smirks and quickly sits.

I walk to my desk, pull out the poetry assignment that was due today and quickly reread it. I wrote it a week ago. Shit. There's no way I want to read this to the class. Not with Zack in the room anyway. When I wrote it I was hurt and sad and it seems like a lifetime ago. I also never thought anyone but Mr. Davis would read it. My thoughts are too personal to share. "Mr. Davis. I don't seem to have the assignment with me," I lie.

Mr. Davis squints and walks to me. He takes the paper I'm feverishly trying to shove in the back of my folder out of my hands and glances down at it. "Here it is." He points to the front of the classroom. "Go. Or sit down and take a zero and Mr. Martin can read his today."

The short walk to the front of the room feels more like I'm walking the plank. I take a deep breath and look to Zack. He's watching me intently with a confused look on his face. I don't look up as I read the words from my page.

> *Shattered like glass.*
> *A million tiny little pieces surround my bare feet.*
> *The sun was shining.*
> *Now clouds loom low in the once bright sky.*
> *I try to move.*
> *But I can't.*
> *The shards that remain cut my feet with every step.*
> *Reminding me.*
> *The birds once sang a song that was music to my ears.*
> *Now my world is silent.*
> *Blood seeps from the wounds inflicted at my feet.*
> *The pain keeps me from walking away.*
> *I wish he had remained silent.*
> *Never let me hear his voice.*
> *Never let me in. Only to push me out.*
> *The blood will dry. Cuts will heal.*
> *The pain will never be forgotten.*

The room is silent when I finish reading. I walk to my seat without looking up and quietly slip in, wishing I could disappear. I feel Zack's eyes on the back of my head from the seat behind me, but I don't have the courage to face him.

Eventually the bell rings. Zack is standing beside my desk before I can even get my books into my backpack.

"Nikki, could you please stay after for a moment?" Mr. Davis calls from the front of the class as the classroom begins to empty. I look to Zack and he appears as stressed as I feel.

"I'll meet you in the parking lot. I'll skip practice today," he says, his voice low.

"I have practice too."

"You're skipping too." His tone tells me it's not something he plans to discuss. I nod and he leaves me with Mr. Davis, a weary look on his face.

Zack opens the car door for me. We're both still quiet when he slips into the driver's seat. The roar of the engine the only sound in the stillness of the car as we pull out of the school parking lot.

"You hungry?"

"Not really."

Zack nods and pulls onto the parkway. He turns the music on to occupy the miles of space that separates us. We drive for a while in silence until he pulls down a road. A lighthouse I've never seen before looms ahead.

"Do you know all the lighthouses in California?" I try to make light of the tension that fills the air.

He smiles. "I looked them up on the internet when you said you liked them. Probably passed them a million times and never even noticed they were there before you."

We walk up the narrow damp stairwell to the top of the lighthouse in silence. Climbing through a small window frame, we sit with our backs against the wall, our feet hanging over the edge. The sound of the waves crashing against the shoreline calms me…or maybe it's the boy sitting next to me.

When he turns to face me, the look on his face is so serious, so intense, it scares me for a minute. He brushes a stray lock of hair that escaped from my braid behind my ear. "I'm so sorry I made you feel that way."

There's pain and sadness in his face. "It's not your fault."

"Yes. It is." His voice grows louder, insistent.

"You were struggling. I get it. You lost someone you loved. I know you said you felt guilty for being happy, but I'm sure it was more than that. It probably felt disloyal to be with me. It's not the same, but sometimes I feel that way with Aunt Claire. We'll have fun just sitting around talking or shopping or something and then I get sad afterwards because I feel like I'm dishonoring my mother. Like I'm letting someone take her place." I pause. "I wrote that poem almost two weeks ago. A lot has changed since then. We've changed. Let's not look backward anymore, let's keep moving forward."

He shakes his head and smiles. "How did I get so lucky to find you? I can't find the words to tell you what I need to say, but here you are, knowing exactly what I was feeling." He's quiet for a long moment before he looks up. "I'm just going to say it one more time, because I need to. I'm so sorry for hurting you."

I smile. "I accept your apology."

"Forward from now on, I promise," Zack says and it looks as if a little of the weight he's been carrying around may have been lightened.

There's a comfortable lull in our conversation and I realize we *both* need to move forward unburdened for this to work. "Umm…Zack. I need to tell you something," I say apprehensively.

His eyes jump to mine in a flash, his face grows anxious. "That doesn't sound good."

I contemplate how to tell him, without revealing just how twisted my life is, but when I look in his eyes, he gives me the strength I need. He tells me that whatever it is, he'll be fine with it, he won't judge me — without ever saying a word. So I take a deep breath and begin. "I have a sister."

Zack's eyebrows jump in surprise. "Okay." He waits for the other shoe to drop.

"Who I've never met." Baby steps.

"Okay." His brows furrow a bit more, but there's still no judgment.

"And I only found out she existed when my mom died."

"Where is she?"

"I don't know. I think she might be here in California."

"Do you want to meet her?"

"More than anything."

"So what's stopping you?"

"I don't know her name or anything about her. Except we're twins. My mom gave her up at birth, because she had health problems. My mom had her own serious health problems, raising me alone was already a challenge."

"And you don't know who the adoptive parents are?"

I nod.

"How do we find out then?" Zack asks.

We. He said *we.* And just like that, the bond between us grows deeper. For the next two hours, I fill him in on all the details. Mom's letter, Ms. Evans, Aunt Claire. All of it.

And when we're all talked out, Zack wraps his arms around me and holds me tight. "Together," he says and I pull back to look at him.

His captivating blue eyes sparkle with the reflection of the blue sea behind him. "We'll find her together. And if she's anything like you, I'm sure I'll love her."

The sun blazes its way down beneath the ocean, refusing to stop beaming its heavenly rays even as it's swallowed by the horizon. We sit quietly and enjoy the view as daylight falls to darkness.

Zack pulls me from sitting next to him to straddled between his open bent knees. Strong arms wrap around my waist, just below my breasts. He kisses the top of my head.

"What's your favorite holiday?"

"Valentine's Day." I say, not having to think about my response. I haven't told him it also happens to be my birthday. Seven more weeks and I'll be eighteen.

"Valentine's Day, huh? Most people would say Christmas or Thanksgiving, I would think."

I shrug. "Not me. What's yours?"

"Valentine's Day."

I smile. "Did you just make that up?"

"Maybe." I can hear the smile in his voice, even though I can't see him. "I sort of like Thanksgiving a lot too."

"Why is that?"

"All-day football, women cooking, and no shopping for presents," he says as if it was the only obvious answer.

"So you're giving all that up and making Valentine's Day your new favorite holiday. Just like that?"

"Yep."

"And why would you do that?"

He takes my chin in his hand and turns my head, planting a soft kiss on my lips. "Because it's your favorite."

"Yes. But think of all those Thanksgiving traditions you'll be giving up in favor of St. Valentine."

Zack rubs his nose up against mine, then kisses all around my lips. "We'll make new traditions. Valentine's Day traditions for just me and you." He kisses me on the lips a few times, then runs his tongue along my bottom lip. I feel the sensation in places other than my mouth.

"New traditions," I whisper.

Zack nods, a glimmer in his eye tells me we're both thinking the same thing even though neither of us says it. "New traditions."

He grins and kisses me chastely on the lips. I only hope we can hold out for seven more weeks and make our first Valentine's Day together special for both of us.

Nikki

I stop in the street in front of Zack's house, bending over, hands on my knees, to catch my breath. That feeling hits me again. It's eerie, like someone is watching me. I wipe the sweat from my forehead, pull the earbud from my ear, and scan the area, finding no one. Then I notice the blinds moving inside the house across the street. *Emily's* house. I stare for a moment, but eventually the blinds still. My own fears and suspicions are definitely getting the best of me.

Zack answers the door before I even press the doorbell. He smiles at me and grabs my hand, yanking me to him. The kiss he plants on my lips makes me forget everything else.

"Were you able to get back into the attic after she left this morning?" Zack asks as soon as the door closes behind me.

I nod, but say nothing, looking around.

"No one's home. My parents went to San Diego to visit my Aunt. They won't be back until late tonight."

"Oh."

"Was it Long Beach Hospital?"

"No, it was North Shore University Hospital. I googled it. It's about twenty miles away."

"I know where it is."

"Their website said you either have to go in person and show ID to request medical records or fill out some forms and get them notarized," I say.

"Do you have your school ID on you?"

"Yes."

"So let's go."

"But..." I look down at my running gear. "I'm a sweaty mess."

"You look hot."

"I am hot. I ran fast and it's warm out today."

Zack wiggles his eyebrows. "That's not what I meant."

"Oh." I blush.

He pulls me close again. "I like you like this."

"With my hair falling out of my ponytail, face flush and sweat dripping from my body?"

He nods, a dirty grin on his face. "You sweaty and flushed is my favorite look for you. It reminds me of two nights ago in your room."

The temperature on my already heated face rises. "You have a one track mind."

"Yep. All Nikki, all the time."

Zack kisses me again and groans. "Come on, let's get on the road, or we won't wind up going anywhere today."

We pass a sign on the highway for North Shore University Hospital and my nerves ratchet up. Zack squeezes the left hand he's been holding since we started driving.

"You okay?" He glances at me and then back to the road.

It was Zack's idea to sneak back into the attic and get the name of the hospital so I could try to get my records. He's been incredible ever since I told him about my sister. Searching online and finding out all about California law. I don't feel like I'm in this alone anymore. "Thank you for taking me."

"You don't have to thank me. We're in this together."

We park and walk to the front door hand in hand. I pause a few seconds as the motion activated front door slides open. Zack looks back. "Hey. You okay? We don't have to do this today if you're not ready."

"I know." I blow out a stream of air. "I'm ready."

The security guard directs us to the Medical Records Department and we follow a series of hallways until we come to the last turn. Zack squeezes my hand reminding me he is here— each step of the way.

"Do you think this is it?" Zack teases as we arrive at a blue door with a ridiculously huge "Medical Records" sign.

"Maybe." I smile and try to sound light, but it's difficult to hide my anxiety.

Zack pulls the door open, holding it for me to walk through first. The rusty hinges squeal a high-pitched creak, catching the attention of the gray haired older woman sitting at one of the desks. Everyone else in the large room ignores us.

"Can I help you?" Her voice is more pleasant than I expected.

I hesitate and Zack jumps in. "Yes, thank you. We'd like to get some medical records."

"Sure." She walks to the table of forms next to us. "Fill out this blue one. I'll also need to make a photocopy of your ID."

With a shaking hand, I complete the request for medical documents, dig my school identification card from my pocket and hand it to the woman. She smiles and examines it. "You were born in 1996."

"Yes." I respond.

195

"That would make you seventeen still, right?"

"Yes, seventeen. I'll be eighteen soon."

"I'm sorry. We can't release your medical records unless you're eighteen. Your parents can authorize the release of the records, if you want to have them come in?"

Zack speaks up on my behalf. "Nikki's parents both passed away. We were hoping to find some information in the file about her sister who was adopted. "

The woman looks at me sadly. "I'm sorry. A guardian perhaps?"

"Aunt Claire?" Zack turns to me and whispers doubtingly.

I return my attention to the woman. "I don't have anyone who can sign." Aunt Claire has records from my birth. She obviously knows I have a sister, yet hasn't said anything. The more time that passes, the more Mom's warning in her letter seems real. I really hoped the warning was part of her paranoia; Aunt Claire turned out to be pretty great otherwise.

"Have you tried Social Services down at City Hall in Long Beach? They might be able to help."

The woman is trying to be kind. I force a smile, but fail miserably. "I haven't had the best experience with social services. I'll come back when I'm eighteen."

The woman nods.

"Thank you for your time," I say.

We're almost out the door when her voice stops us. "Wait." She comes to the door and extends her arm to a row of seats. "Give me a minute. I have a friend at Social Services. Let me make a call for you." She winks and goes back to her desk to use the phone.

A few minutes later she returns and hands me a slip of paper. "Here's my friend's name and number. She searched the system and you're in there. She's going to have your file pulled. She said it could take a few months to get the files from archives, but she'll call you when they come in."

"Thank you for all your help," Zack says warmly. "It was very nice of you to go out of your way and make that call for us."

"I hope you find what you're looking for. If they don't call, you come back after you turn eighteen and ask for Marcy. I'll help you sort through the documents to find what you need."

"Thank you."

The woman was kind. But, nonetheless, I feel disappointed as we leave.

Zack wraps his arm around me as we snake our way through the maze of hallways. "We'll keep looking. There has to be something somewhere. There just has to be." He squeezes me close.

Just as we reach the front door, Zack stops abruptly. A handsome older man in a suit is walking towards us.

"Zack? What are you doing here?" The man asks, friendly but a hint of concern in his voice.

"I'm…helping a friend. But we're done now. It was good to see you." Zack's words are polite, but his action is rude. He slowed, but never stopped, even though the man had clearly stopped to talk.

"Who was that, Zack? Why did you rush us away so quickly?" I ask when we're out of hearing distance.

"Just a friend of my parents. Nobody important. I didn't want to explain or answer any questions. Your business isn't anyone else's business." He plants a kiss on my forehead. "Let's go home."

I turn back to the front entrance as we reach the door. The man is still standing at the door, watching us.

Chapter 33

Zack

Six weeks have passed since the day Nikki read the poem that bared her broken heart to the class. And I've made it my mission to make it up to her everyday. Each day gets better and better. Instead of finding things that I don't like as we grow even closer, I discover more to love about her. We've become practically inseparable the last few weeks. Even at night. The nights her Aunt works at the hospital, I stay till morning. My parents are so delirious I'm happy, they don't even care that I don't come home a few nights each week. Plus, I'm eighteen now.

Although my parents may not care, her Aunt Claire would most definitely have something to say about it. I get the odd feeling she doesn't like me, although Nikki insists she's just overprotective. Either way, there's no way I'm getting caught when she gets home in two hours. My alarm goes off at six and I slip out of bed, trying my best not to wake Nikki. Then I realize that she never put her shirt back on last night.

Morning wood and the sight of her bare, beautiful breasts, and I push aside the notion that I have to let her get some rest, even though we were up half the night fooling around. Each time it gets harder and harder to stop ourselves. But at least we both know there's relief in the not so distant future.

We've agreed to wait till Valentines' Day to be together for the first time. Nikki has no idea it was Emily's birthday, and at first I was hesitant to think of spending the day making love to someone else. But the night she suggested it, I would have agreed to anything to keep that beautiful smile on her face.

Lowering myself back to the bed, I crawl up her body, positioning myself over her. I kiss her neck first, until she groans, waking from her sleep without complaint. She wraps her arms around my back and her nails dig in as my mouth grazes her collarbone. A quiet moan escapes her lips and the sound makes me crazy. My kisses become more adamant, harsher, faster, more consuming. I kiss her everywhere except the place we've deemed off limits for now, taking my time as I make my way from the tops of her toes back to her neck.

She groans as I hover over her, our needy body parts perfectly aligned. Wrapping her legs around my back, she pulls me even closer against her. The sensation is incredible. My hardness pushes deeply into her. I feel the throb of both our bodies, even through two layers of underwear.

"Tell me again why we're waiting," I groan as I dip my tongue into her mouth with need. My fingers press into her hips, and I roll us so she's on top. There's something so fucking sexy about watching her take control. And she does. She kisses me and then moves down to my neck, nipping at the end of each kiss. It drives me goddamn wild. Then she moves lower. Returning the worship I've just extolled up and down her body, she lowers her mouth to my chest, kissing my pectoral muscles. But the position is more than I can tolerate. Her bare breasts are pushed up against my hardness and my body begins to rock into her before I even catch myself.

"Nikki," I breathe. She looks up at me, her eyes hooded and seductive and I know I can't possibly last like this. Startling her, I flip her back over to her back and kiss her chastely on the lips before jumping up from the bed.

"Zack," she gasps, looking as dejected as I feel.

"I have to go." I search around frantically for my sweat pants.

"Ugghhh…," she groans and pulls the sheet over her head.

I throw on my sweats, pull my t-shirt over my head and kiss her through the sheet. "I'll call you later. Get dressed before your Aunt comes home."

She tosses a pillow at my back as I grab my shoes and practically run out the door.

The mall is a place I utterly detest. Correction. The mall is a place I utterly detest…without Keller. Standing on line at the pretzel stand thirty feet away from the men's room, I hear his voice boom through the bathroom door.

"Corn! When did I eat corn?" he screams, his deep voice impossible not to hear.

Every guy in front of me in line cracks up. Every girl crinkles up her nose and looks totally disgusted. He emerges a minute later, all smiles as he raises his hands above his head to display them to everyone in line. "Clean! I washed 'em this time," he exclaims, as if it's a novel feat.

I shake my head and order.

"Dude, no wonder you don't have a girlfriend. You're disturbed."

"It's all part of my selection process." Keller taps his finger to his temple, indicating how smart he is.

"I'm afraid to ask."

Keller smiles. "If a chick can't laugh at my jokes, she's not for me." He shrugs.

"So you're waiting for a girl to think you're funny, rather than disgusting?"

"Yep," Keller says proudly.

I chuckle. "Great plan."

"I thought so."

"You're going to be alone for a long time, jackass."

"Nikki laughs at my jokes," he grins. "*And* she's smoking hot."

"Stop looking at my girlfriend."

"What should I do, cover my eyes whenever I see her?" he goads me.

"You know what I mean. Stop looking at her like *that*."

"I don't think I can. She's got some ass, man." Keller mimes a shapely ass with his hands.

If it was anyone else in the world, they'd be laid out on the floor right now, admitting that they are openly ogling my girlfriend. But Keller...well...he's just Keller. So I wind up and punch him in the arm, hard enough to leave a bruise, but falling short of beating the crap out of him.

"Oww!" Keller rubs his arm. "What did you do that for?"

Clueless. Totally clueless. We walk the mall for another hour in search of the perfect Valentine's Day gift for Nikki, but nothing seems to be right. We stop at the last jewelry store in the mall. The sales clerk looks perplexed when Keller asks her, with a completely straight face, if she can direct him to their lingerie department. Luckily, Keller sees some guys from the team outside of the store and I get a few minutes to look around without being kicked out of yet another store.

"Who are you looking to buy a gift for today?" The saleswoman asks hesitantly.

"My girlfriend."

"For Valentine's Day?"

"Yeah."

"Are you looking for anything in particular?"

"No. I guess I'm just hoping something jumps out at me."

The young salesclerk smiles. "Tell me a little about her, maybe it will give me an idea to help point you in the right direction."

"She doesn't really wear a lot of jewelry. Well, sometimes she wears these beads. But they're not really fancy jewelry, she just wears them because they were her Mom's." I look around and everything just seems too formal and cold to give Nikki. "To be honest, I'm not even sure if jewelry is the right gift for her," I admit with a defeated shrug.

"She wears her Mom's beads? Did her Mother pass away?"

"Yeah, last year."

"Hmmm." She looks around the store. "Maybe I have an idea."

She walks away for a moment and comes back with a black velvet tray. A long gold chain hangs delicately on it, a large pretty heart weighing down the bottom. She sets it down in front of me. "It's an antique, so it's a little different than most that you see today." She presses something at the side of the heart and it opens. "It's a locket. There's room for two pictures. Maybe you could put a picture of her Mom on one side and you on the other." She turns the heart over. "The back is inscribable, you could even write her a little note."

A heart to represent her favorite holiday, a place for a picture of her Mother and me *and* room to leave her a note. "I'll take it."

Chapter 34

Nikki

N ervousness and excitement mix for a potent cocktail. Not unlike my limited dabbling with alcohol, this cocktail leaves me nauseous and ready to throw up. I'll never be able to sleep tonight.

My phone rings and I smile at the goofy selfie that comes up, indicating it's Ashley. We took the picture on my last day in Texas. We're both lying in the grass, our long hair splayed all around us as we look up, smiling widely for the camera. It was about one heartbeat after we snapped the shot that Ashley realized she had a huge Texas size spider crawling on her face. The picture captured that short second where she was still smiling, yet the spider appears prominently on her check. Absolutely priceless.

"Got any plans for Valentine's Day?" she asks, teasing. Over the last month we've gone from talking twice a week to hour-long deep conversations every single day. Sometimes more than once. She knows how anxious I am about tomorrow.

"Valentine's Day? Nah. I was thinking maybe I'd stay in, snuggle up with a good book," I quietly close the door to my room.

Aunt Claire is home and I don't want her overhearing my conversation with Ashley.

"I think I might be more excited about you doing the dirty deed than you are. You sound so calm." Every time I talk to Ash she has a different name for sex. Today's isn't terrible, but in the last week we've had makin bacon, rockin the trailer, bumping uglies and my personal favorite, one I still don't even understand, roasting the broomstick.

"I'm far from calm. Every morning I wake up panicked about something that could go wrong. Today I envisioned myself throwing up on him before the bacon even made it into the frying pan." I plop down on my bed on my stomach. My face is so close to my pillow, I can smell Zack, his shampoo leaving behind a scent I've come to associate with him in my bed. I take a deep whiff and smile as I exhale.

"What are you doing?"

"Nothing," I lie.

"Did you just sniff something?"

"No!"

"Liar. What did you smell?"

"Ugh…." I growl because she knows me so well. "My pillow," I confess.

"Smells like Zack?"

"Yes, if you must know."

"I must." We both laugh. Aunt Claire would definitely be upset if she knew I hadn't washed my pillowcases in weeks. But I just can't bear to give up the smell. It keeps me company when he slips out from my bed in the morning.

We talk for a while. She tells me about a new guy she's dating, yet doesn't really like, and I tell her more about school and last night with Zack. He took me to another lighthouse to watch the sunset. The sixth one we've visited so far.

"So did you buy anything special to wear tomorrow night?" Ashley asks.

"Aunt Claire bought me a cute sundress I haven't worn yet, so I thought I'd wear it. It's blue, Zack's favorite color."

"I was talking about what you planned to wear under the sundress."

Panic sets in. I hadn't even given any thought to wearing any special underwear. "Oh my god. I didn't even think about that! Am I supposed to wear something special for the first time? Like a teddy or something?"

"Calm down. I don't think there are any set rules. I just thought you might have since it's been such a big buildup to the day."

The nerves I had temporarily been able to set aside for the last ten minutes, come back blindingly strong. "You're right. It has been a big build up. What happens if it isn't what we expect it to be?"

"What do you expect it to be?"

"I don't know. Special. Emotional, I guess."

"Well, what you wear has nothing to do with any of that. So I wouldn't worry about it."

Aunt Claire knocks on my door to tell me it's time for dinner. "I have to go," I say to Ash. "I'll call you tomorrow."

"Right after you fornicate."

"Fornicate? Someone's been reading the dictionary."

"Do you like riding the baloney pony better?"

"Stick with fornicate."

"If you insist."

"I'll call you tomorrow."

"Can't wait."

The smell of Belgian waffles wafts through the air the next morning, the corners of my mouth turning upwards before I even open an eye. Aunt Claire knows they're my favorite. I'd never had homemade waffles before coming to California. Honestly, I'm not even sure I realized you could make them at home, no less make them taste as incredible as she does.

I pad through the house, my feet shuffling sleepily on the floor, even though my senses are wide awake from the smell.

"Happy Birthday, sleepyhead! And Happy Valentine's Day!" Aunt Claire smiles as I enter the kitchen.

I eat one waffle, then half of a second, poking with my fork at the rest. It hits me how strange it's been to have someone cooking all the time for me. A stove in a trailer isn't quite the same as the one Aunt Claire has. Plus, Mom wasn't much of a cook anyway. She never ate much, she thought if we had unexpired milk and Cheerios all was golden. Dinners generally consisted of frozen food thawed in the oven or fast food. None of it good for Mom's diabetes, but she was always stubborn. Even when I started working in a supermarket in the months before she died and I'd bring home fresh fruit or vegetables, Mom would say she wasn't hungry.

Aunt Claire must spot me drifting into a sad place thinking of Mom because she jumps up from her chair like a puppy that spotted a treat, exclaiming, "I almost forgot your presents! Stay right there!" and disappears to her room in a flurry.

I'm hit with a pang of guilt when she rushes back in with a pile of beautifully wrapped presents— more than I've ever received at once before. She's rushing to cook for me and give me gifts before school, and I'm keeping a major secret from her. Today I feel more guilt than I have in the past few months. Maybe it's because I'm wondering if someone made my sister a special breakfast for her birthday. A sister I pretend to know nothing about to Aunt Claire. Each day my dishonesty gets harder and harder.

Aunt Claire piles the boxes at my feet. They're dripping with curled ribbons and bows and wrapped in red shiny paper covered in pink hearts to commemorate my Valentine's birthday.

"Open them!" she insists as I'm inspecting the beautiful packages. She shoves the first of the larger boxes onto my lap. Somehow she always seems to know when I'm overwhelmed with emotions that make me uncomfortable, drawing me back into a conversation and away from the awkward mental space I'm stuck in.

There are three boxes of the same size and then one very small box that has me the most curious. I want to rush at the small one first, but instead I open them as Aunt Claire hands them to me. Clearly, she is building drama.

Inside box number one, I find a beautiful teal green dress I had stopped to look at on a mannequin at Bloomingdales when Aunt Claire and I were shopping at the mall last week. The color drew my attention at first. The shade of teal looked like water in a Caribbean beach photograph. Beyond the color I fell in love with the row of tiny white shiny pearls lining the scoop neck of the dress. I'm not a particularly "girly girl" but this dress was stunning and I couldn't help think about what Zack might think if he saw me in it.

"Aunt Claire, I didn't even know you saw me looking at this dress." I'm kind of speechless. I've never had a dress this expensive before. "You shouldn't have. You do so much for me already."

A tear wells in Aunt Claire's eye and without thinking I spring to my feet and hug her. "Thank you. I love it. It's the most beautiful dress I have ever seen," I say running my finger over the precious pearls that had caught my eye.

I hold it up examining the plunging back that is also lined with little pearls. "It's like something off the cover of a magazine," I say still staring at it with disbelief that it's really mine.

"You're going to look like you belong on the cover of a magazine, Nikki. You're a beautiful girl and this dress is going to be sensational on you. It's a little dressy but I thought maybe you could

209

wear it tonight for your date with Zack— you only turn 18 once. I know how much you're looking forward to it." She winks. "Not that you've given me too many details."

I grin. "Zack will be speechless. Well, at least I hope he will." I say. "He has plans to take me to a special dinner. I'm not sure where. He wants it all to be a surprise."

"Well it must be a little overwhelming for Zack with your birthday and your first Valentine's Day together all at once," she muses. "I bet he's worried trying to get everything just right."

"I didn't tell him it was my birthday," I admit, realizing how crazy that actually is.

"What? Why?" Aunt Claire asks with sincere shock in her voice.

I lie. I really want to confide in Aunt Claire, but I can't tell her our plans for tonight are enough pressure on us. "I don't want too much pressure on him, Valentine's Day is hard enough." I shrug, trying my best to come off casual.

I open the next two boxes to find new running gear. Three light-weight, bright, fun colored Nike running shirts in box number one and three Nike running shirts and a sports bra in the other. Aunt Claire really is thoughtful. She's learned my taste precisely. The gifts are exactly what I would have picked.

As I'm holding up my new shorts to feel how feather light they are, Aunt Claire hands me the tiny box I have been eyeing all along.

"This one is special. There's a story to go with it. Open it," Aunt Claire says quietly.

I peel the shiny red paper off to find a tiny white quilted jewelry box. Feelings overwhelm me once again. "Aunt Claire, you shouldn't have…I mean it."

She cuts me off before I can express that she's done too much. "Open it, Nikki. That's an order," She smiles, her eyes excited with anticipation.

Inside the box is a beautiful white gold ring with two heart-shaped sapphire stones abutting one another. The sapphire hearts are lined completely with tiny round diamonds. I'm speechless. I've never even been this close to such an exquisite piece of jewelry, much less had someone give me a gift this expensive.

I don't remove the ring from the box. "I can't, Aunt Claire. I really can't," I say, my voice trembling with emotion. I'm overwhelmed by guilt. I don't deserve a gift like this. I used her, coming to live with her only to find my sister. I don't deserve this generous gift. I don't deserve any of it.

"I told you there was a story. The ring was my mother's. Your grandmother Anne's ring. My father had it made for her as a gift and gave it to her the day your mother was born. I was born on September 15th, three years before your mother was born. Your mom was due on September 18th. When your grandfather learned he was going to have a second September baby he had this ring made to celebrate the two babies. Sapphires are the birthstone for September. Your mother always loved this ring. When we were little, she and I used to take it from our mother's jewelry box and try it on, pretending we were princesses."

Aunt Claire continues before I can find any words to speak, "You never got to know your grandmother, and your mother loved this ring. I thought it would be something special for you to have. They are both watching over you now from heaven, Nikki. I thought you might feel like you have a piece of your mom's memories with this ring." She's still smiling, but a tear runs down her cheek.

"I don't know anything about my grandmother. I've been afraid to ask too many questions," I admit without thinking, my own tears falling to match hers.

"You don't have to be afraid to ask questions. I'm just afraid to overwhelm you with too much information. We have plenty of time for you to learn about the family you didn't know. There's no need to rush."

For a moment I forget the ring box still sitting gingerly in the palm of my hand and worry Aunt Claire somehow found out about my plans to find my sister. Her words seem to be a plea not to push for information too fast. Or maybe it's just my own guilt.

"I'm sorry, Nikki. We don't need to be so serious on your birthday. It's a happy day. You're eighteen, it's Valentine's Day, you have a beautiful new dress and a big date!" She turns the mood from somber to light— one of her best pseudo parenting skills.

Aunt Claire takes the box from me and removes the breathtaking ring. She places it on my right ring finger in one quick slip— so fast I can't even resist. She holds my hand out and says, "Perfect. I knew it would be."

Amazingly, it fits as if it was made for me. I think about how Mom must have felt as a little girl, running around pretending to be a princess. It is truly a moment of both sadness and joy. I will never be able to understand how those emotions can run in such a tight parallel inside one heart.

"You don't have to wear it to school if you're worried about losing it. Save it and wear it on your big date tonight. Actually, we better hurry up now or you'll be late to school," Aunt Claire says rushing to clear the breakfast plates as I fold the shiny red wrapping paper and put it into the boxes to save.

"Aunt Claire? She turns. "Yes?"

"Thank you. Thank you for everything," I say, and hug her.

Chapter 35

Zack

I'm happy Mom isn't in the kitchen when I come downstairs early this morning. She would definitely be nosing into my business if she found me up an hour before normal.

I riffle through the kitchen drawers where Mom keeps some sewing supplies, finding the scissors I'm searching for. Just as I grab them and turn to head back upstairs, Mom switches on the light. Damn.

"Is everything okay, Zack? Why are you up so early?" I hear the nervousness in her voice. It's been nine months since Emily's accident and even though I'm back at school and dating Nikki, Mom still worries every time she sees me alone and quiet. Today more so than any other day because of the giant pink elephant she is no doubt fretting over— Emily's 18th birthday would have been today. Nobody has said a word about it and I'm thankful for that. I'm trying to focus on Nikki and our special night, even though guilt shifted into my brain as I woke this morning.

"Everything is fine, Mom. I was just looking for a scissors. No worries, it's just for wrapping a present."

"Oh, Valentine's Day. You bought a present for Nikki?" Mom asks, the familiar sound of parental inquisition in her voice.

"Yes. Couldn't really go out tonight without a present, could I? You raised me better than that," I kiss her on the cheek, which I know will make her happy.

"Well, I'm a very good gift wrapper if you need my help." Mom is definitely not letting it go without seeing this present. I relent and pull the black satin necklace box out of my pocket and show it to her.

Mom opens the box and eyes the locket. "It's beautiful, Zack." Her voice is full of emotion. "Nikki will love it. I'm so glad you found someone like her, sweetie. You deserve to be happy."

"There are spots for two pictures inside. I thought Nikki could put one of herself and one of her mom so they would be together over her heart whenever she wears it," I explain, myself getting a little choked up with emotion.

"Nikki is a strong girl. I can tell. It takes a very resilient person to get through losing a parent at such a young age. You and Nikki have a bond because of..." Mom stops. She hasn't said Emily's name since the funeral ended. Dad hasn't either. They're both afraid of opening a floodgate of emotions with just that one word.

"Emily," I say finishing Mom's sentence. "Nikki knows about Emily, Mom. I told her one night out at the Point soon after we met. You're right. I think it is part of our bond. We both lived through something that most people can't understand."

"You're so grown up now, Zack," Mom says with both pride and sadness in her voice. "You shouldn't have had to grow up so fast, but we can't change that. And, over the last few months, I've seen what a caring, thoughtful and mature man you've become. I'm very proud of who you are and how you've handled the last year, Zack."

There are no words. None that I can say right now anyway. I hug Mom tightly and ask her if she'll help wrap the present. "Your crazy perfectionism comes in handy every once in a while," I laugh and hand her the scissors.

After Mom returns from the wrapping paper closet in her craft room she settles in at the table with five different appropriate wrapping papers for me to choose from. "Pick one," Mom demands in her happiest insistent voice.

"Hallmark has less options than you do." But I actually spend a few minutes surveying the papers to pick the right one. I really do want everything to be perfect tonight.

When Mom cuts the paper and starts wrapping, I'm relieved she didn't take the locket out of the box and turn it over to read the inscription I had engraved on the back. I wouldn't have stopped her, but I would have been a little embarrassed.

Love needs no words.
You had me before you even spoke.

I would have to explain the meaning to Mom. Those wordless first meetings between Nikki and me are private— intimate, something that belongs between just us.

The gift looks beautiful. Mom spent ten minutes curling pink ribbon with the edge of the scissors to add the final finish. I grab the gift, kiss Mom once again and head upstairs to get ready.

Before I hit the top of the stairs, Mom asks, "Does she know today is…" I don't make her finish.

"No, Mom I don't want Nikki to know it's Emily's birthday. Not now. There's no reason. It would only hurt her and spoil a day that's important to her. So, no. I'm not telling her," I take the last two steps up, leaving her no time to offer her thoughts.

"Enjoy your day, Zack," Mom calls as I run out the front door a little while later. "I love you."

"Love you too," I shout back.

As I settle into the driver's seat of the Charger, I turn my phone on and find five missed calls from Nikki.

Nikki

I'm not really sure why I took the bus. I run more than this distance every day. I guess I wanted to look mature and professional when I arrived.

The large, old, city bus stops directly in front of Long Beach City Hall. Half the bus gets off with me. It's just before nine and people are rushing into work at the row of office buildings that line the street. I stand staring at the building, trying to decide whether I should go in or not.

My legs tremble, I'm doubtful I can even make the few steps to the front door. I wish Zack had answered. Right about now, I'm thinking waiting for him would've been a better idea, but I wasn't thinking when I answered the call. About to walk into school, I took out my phone to turn it off just as it rang. I nearly dropped the phone when the social worker told me my records had arrived and I could make an appointment to see them.

"When is the next appointment?" I asked.

"I have Tuesday the twenty-eighth at eleven." *Two weeks*, I thought. I won't sleep for that long knowing the answers are so close.

"You don't have anything sooner?"

"We're booked solid. Unless you can get here in a half hour. We had a cancellation this morning at nine."

So here I am. Alone. Possibly about to find out about my sister— on our birthday. The day I've been anxiously anticipating for months, yet now that it's finally here, I'm tempted to put it off. Will I view my life the same way when I walk back out today?

I almost turn around and run twice before I finally reach the door. I enter the slow moving glass revolving door, nearly forgetting to exit as it circles into the building lobby. The large gray atrium looks a lot like the many government offices I've entered during the last eighteen years. A few vases of plastic flowers are the only decoration to warm the bland industrial feel.

It seems like a lifetime ago I sat in the worn green pleather chairs inside the Texas government offices waiting hours for Mom to be called to reapply for food stamps or our housing vouchers. Mom always received public assistance to help raise me because of her poor health— both mental and physical. Life was hard. I understand that more now than when I lived it. But I guess that's always the case, somehow it's easier to look back than to see what's right before your eyes.

I walk toward the reception desk, thinking about how much my life has changed in the last nine months. I feel guilty realizing life has changed for the better. If only it had changed like this when Mom was still here.

The receptionist is busy talking on the phone and not at all interested in looking up to greet me as I reach the desk. She knows I'm here. I saw her eyes look up just enough to spot me and ignore me just as quickly. She continues on her personal call for several more minutes leaving me standing here contemplating turning around and walking out.

Nerves keep me glued in place, I'm unable to turn and leave, yet I'm also terrified to stay. Finally, the cranky receptionist hangs up the phone and turns her eyes upon me. "Can I help you?" she says in a tone that tells me she doesn't exactly love her job.

"I have an appointment," I respond in a voice that is barely audible. Fear has set in.

"You and everybody else, honey. Look around. You ain't the only one. What department?" she barks.

"Social Work. I'm here to look at some records," I explain as if she might be listening.

She's not. "Social Work. Sign the book and sit in the area with the orange chairs," She points to the far right corner of the atrium.

Turning to follow her finger, I find that, while there are a dozen people sitting in the green chair area, the orange seats are bodiless. Lucky me, I guess. I head to the putrid seats and sit down. At least I'm sitting in a new color these days.

Looking around the room, the green chairs are mostly full of women with small children. The bored toddlers hang on their mothers or roll around on the floor at their sides. It must be the area to wait for public assistance, an area I know well. My heart aches for the children sitting there, their moms probably have it rough. I instantly feel six years old again.

Before my mind can drift too deeply back to sadder times, a woman calls out, "Nicole. Nicole Fallon." I almost miss my name because nobody calls me Nicole. I didn't even sign in as Nicole.

My legs are weak with fear as I stand to approach the young woman calling my name. I raise my hand to motion I'm here, because at the moment words fail me. She greets me halfway.

"Hi Nicole. I'm Valerie Hawkins. We spoke on the phone this morning." I spot a file in her hand labeled *Nicole Fallon*. My heart races wondering if that folder contains the name of my sister.

"Yes, I remember. Thank you for seeing me Ms. Hawkins. I'm a little nervous," I confide in her. Something I'm sure she spots without being told.

"I understand. People usually are. It's normal. Let's go to my office." Ms. Hawkins leads the way down a narrow hall. The walls are not the cold sterile gray of the atrium but an ugly, depressing hospital pale blue. No pictures attempt to dress up the walls, which are stained and chipped from many people who have leaned against them. The décor matches the mood of the occupants— both the visitors and most of the employees.

Ms. Hawkins opens a wood door at the end of the hall with an old gold doorplate that reads, *Long Beach Department of Social Work.* The office is crammed with cubicles full of workers. I hope Ms. Hawkins has a private office somewhere, but quickly find out otherwise as she ushers me into a cubicle not far from the entrance door.

"Have a seat, Nicole." She pulls out a chair holding a pile of files and looks around for a place to put them, but every surface is already stacked high with bulging files. Setting the heap down on the floor, she positions the empty chair next to her desk so I can sit facing her.

"It's Nikki. Nobody has ever called me Nicole. My mom liked Nikki better." I tuck my hands under my thighs to hide the trembling. My head is light, the room spins a bit and it's entirely possible I could actually be sick. I do my best to steady myself as Ms. Hawkins opens her desk drawer and takes out a second folder, which she opens.

"I just need to see your identification, Nikki." She looks up and smiles to make sure I hear her say Nikki, rather than Nicole. She's already more attentive than Ms. Evans.

She inspects my identification, smiles and looks up at me warmly. "Happy Birthday. Eighteen is a big one. Hard to imagine it was ten years ago for me. Enjoy it. Time goes fast." She thumbs through the file and then folds her hands on top of it. "So what kind of information did you hope to find out today?" she cuts to the chase, politely but directly.

"I really don't know anything about my childhood in California. I grew up in Texas. I've only been back in California since my mother died. I came to live with my Aunt who I hadn't even known existed before that." I've told nearly my whole life story to a stranger in five seconds.

"Okay, well your file has your hospital birth records. And it also has some records of Court hearings on visitation," Ms. Hawkins explains.

Visitation? Visitation with who? "I'm not sure I understand."

"Let's start with your birth records. Would that be okay?" she asks, trying to take things slower.

"Yes, I think that would be good. Thank you."

She slides the thicker of the two folders toward me on the desk. "Do you want me to go through it with you or would you rather have a few minutes alone to go through it?" I'm grateful for the choice and tell her I'd like to have a few minutes alone.

"I'll be just across the room using another phone to catch up on some messages. Let me know if you need me," she says as she walks away, leaving me still sitting on my hands.

I reach for the folder, my unsteady hand shaking. My anxiety level surges as I open it. The page fastened to the inside left is a hospital admission form. *Baby Girl B*

I turn slowly through my birth records, learning Baby Girl B— me— was a healthy baby. Three days in the hospital and discharged to "Mother".

The records are scant. I'm not sure what I expected but somehow I thought I would learn more.

I remember Ms. Hawkins saying there were also records of Court orders. I slide the second folder across the desk hoping that something about Baby Girl A is to be found. The large stack of papers are secured with a rubber band. The first page is a faded seventeen year old Court order dated three days after my first birthday. A narrative appears below the date:

> *After a hearing and evidence presented by both parties, this Court orders that Respondent is permitted visitation with his infant daughter, Nicole Fallon, on alternate Sundays from 9 a.m. to 5 p.m. within the county of Long Beach.*
>
> *It is further ordered that Respondent pay child support in the amount of $880.00 per month to the infant's mother, Carla Fallon, through the Office of Child Support Collections.*
>
> *It is acknowledged that based on Respondent's current salary of $116,000.00, the presumptive child support amount under the Federal Child Support Standards Act would be $1355.00 per month. However, a downward departure in support is warranted due to the fact that Respondent and his spouse are the parents of two additional minor children. The Court takes into further consideration the fact that Respondent's custodial daughter, Emily Bennett, born February 14th, 1996, has considerable current medical expenses due to medical complications after birth last year.*
>
> *The Court suggests to the parties that they work towards developing a relationship between these currently estranged siblings.*
>
> *So Ordered:*
>
> *February 17, 1997.*
>
> *Justice Robert Brown*

Emily Bennett? Emily Bennett born February 14, 1996? It has to be a cruel coincidence. There must be other Emily Bennetts in Long Beach. And who is Respondent? I thought my father was dead? *The court directs the parties to work at developing a relationship between the two estranged siblings?*

Suddenly I find it hard to breathe. The air is thick and my lungs can't inhale enough oxygen. If I sit here another minute, I'm certain I'll pass out. I spot Ms. Hawkins on the phone but know I can't afford to wait another moment. Tearing the page from the file, I take off running, heading desperately for the main entrance.

Air. I need air.

When my feet finally reach the concrete out front, I gasp, swallowing down as much oxygen as I can take in. Bent over, hands on my knees, I inhale deeply and exhale loudly, my lungs burn, starving after being deprived. I look up towards the street. There's a bus pulling up I could hop on. But I know I can't possibly enter another confined space. So, I run.

And run.

And run.

Eventually I collapse. Out of breath and panting on the ground, I look up and realize where my feet have lead me. Roselawn Memorial Cemetery. Allie had once told me Zack had been found here lying at Emily's grave several times in the weeks after her death. My heart tightened in my chest each time Aunt Claire and I drove past it, reminding me of what he must have been through.

Sitting trying to catch my breath I tell myself that it won't be what I think. It can't be. My sister is *alive*. My sister is *not* Zack's Emily.

When I finally have enough breath to walk, I compose myself and walk to the small brick office building just beyond the gate. A kind looking old man sitting at the desk reading the newspaper looks up as I enter. "Can I help you, Miss?"

"I'm trying to find someone. A grave site, I mean. I'm here to visit a friend who has passed. Can you tell me how to find the spot?" I ask, my voice breaking more with each word.

"I can help you. Give me the name and year of death and I can search our system," he offers.

"Emily Bennett. She died last year." Just saying the words aloud, tears well up in my eyes.

He punches some keys on his computer. "Got it. J-117. Here's a grounds map. It's not far. You can walk it if you want." He gets up to point the direction from the door and trace the map with his finger for me.

Five minutes later, I'm standing at a row of headstones with a marker "J". I walk past J-1 and look down the long row realizing I'm only a few hundred feet away from the answer. Tiny drops of rain begin to fall as I take the first step down row J. The drops increase both in size and number as I make my way passed J-51, 52.... The rain washes away the tears that have been streaming down my face since I saw the first headstone. Emily can't have been born on Valentine's Day. Please, God, let her birthday be any other day.

In the distance I see a figure placing flowers on a grave as the rain pummels his silhouette. I stop in my tracks. "Long Beach High Football" is emblazed in red letters on the back of his gray sweatshirt— the sweatshirt I have worn so many times.

I quietly slide down behind a large headstone and bow my head to my lap. I can't see Zack now. I don't want to see anyone. I just want to see that grave.

Minutes feel like hours, but eventually he walks away, head down. The walk of grief. I feel sick.

I make my way down to the place where he stood, rain showering my body and blurring my vision as I read the headstones I pass. Then I see the lilies. Fresh, beautiful lilies. Two bundles— each placed in the standing vases on stakes in the wet ground on opposite ends of the headstone. Two visitors were here today.

I kneel in the fresh muddy ground in front of the stone so the rain doesn't impair my vision.

EMILY LYNNE BENNETT

2/14/1996 — 3/27/2013
Beloved daughter of Michael and Lynne Bennett
Beloved Sister of Brent Jon Bennett
Our Angel has been called to Heaven

My body collapses on the grass in front of her grave. I've lost everything at once. Again.

Nikki

"Why are you here?" A woman's voice startles me. I lift my head, wiping the dripping hair plastered to my face from my eyes.

It's *her.*

"Why are you here?" she repeats more insistently when I don't respond.

Who is *she?*

"Why did you come here?" Her stern voice rises.

"Who are you?" Ignoring her question, I finally find my voice.

"I'm Lynne Bennett."

Eyes wide, my head whips to read the headstone again. I turn back to face her, she's staring at me blankly. I have so many questions, yet I don't know what to say.

"I'll ask you again. Why are you here?"

"Emily was my sister."

"Emily didn't have a sister. You and your delusional mother are nothing to Emily."

"But…"

The woman speaks over me. "My husband never loved your mother. She was nothing more than a manipulative young girl."

"I don't understand."

"You don't belong here. You can't take her place. He will never love you."

"Who? Who won't love me?"

"You can't replace her. Not to my husband. Not to Zack. You should have just kept running that day."

"Zack? Zack doesn't even know I'm Emily's sister."

The woman laughs maniacally. "You're as crazy as your mother was. Do you really believe he doesn't know who you are? He's using you. He misses my daughter. I see him running with you, just like he used to do with my Emily. He was so in love with her, so desperate to keep her with him, he turned to a cheap copy. He doesn't give a damn about you."

"I…"

"You should go back to your trailer park. There is nothing here for you."

I stare at her; she doesn't so much as blink. My clothes are muddied and dripping wet. Yet, this woman, standing holding her umbrella, doesn't have a hair out of place or a drop of water on her. I look like the trash she thinks I am.

"Leave!" I jump when she screams. Her blank, perfectly made-up face twists with contempt.

"Leave!" She throws a large bouquet of lilies tied with a white ribbon at me. They hit my face and fall, scattering all around Emily's grave.

I turn, taking one last look at my sister's headstone, then run, never looking back.

I ring the doorbell for the third time, but no one answers. Zack's car isn't here. The driveway is empty. I feel sick. Confused. Angry. Scared. *Lost*. I need to hear Zack tell me she was lying. He couldn't possibly have known Emily was my sister.

I bang on the door. Maybe the bell isn't working. But no one answers. I turn, stopping in my tracks at the sight of Emily's house. My *sister's* house.

Then suddenly I'm ringing the Bennett's doorbell, yet I don't even remember crossing the street.

I wait, but no one answers.

I try the door handle. It's locked.

I need to go inside, although I'm not even sure why.

I try the side door, but it's locked too.

I keep walking; the gate to the backyard is open.

The back door is locked, so I move to the sliding glass patio door.

It opens.

I step just inside the door. I'm not even sure why I'm here.

The house is quiet. I take a few steps. Photos on the fireplace mantel catch my eye. There's one of a girl in a cheerleading outfit, her legs in a wide split mid-air. Long, thick, blonde wavy hair—perfectly tanned skin. *Emily. My sister.* We don't look anything alike. She doesn't have our mother's eyes.

I wander through the house, uncertain of what I'm looking for, what I'm even doing here, until I find it upstairs. *Emily's room.*

It looks like it hasn't been touched since…

There are clothes strewn haphazardly on the bed. I pick up one of the dresses and hold it against me. We're the same size.

Scanning the room, I find the wall behind me littered with photos. There are hundreds of them. All tilted in different directions, random words cut out from magazines and added to the collage. *Cheer. Love. LOL. Prada. Family. PLL.* My eyes seize on the biggest word. Thick pink block letters, in all caps. *ZACK.*

229

I study the pictures.

Emily and her friends.

Emily and her parents.

Emily and Zack.

Dozens and dozens of Emily and Zack.

There must be a hundred of them.

At school.

At dances.

Zack in his football uniform.

Emily in her cheerleading outfit.

I feel sick.

One particular photo catches my eye. It's of Zack and Emily as kids, they couldn't be more than eight or nine. Dirty faces, both smiling wildly, Zack is peddling a bright yellow bike, Emily is on the handlebars.

My head is spinning.

I study their faces. They look so happy.

The wall of pictures begins to blur, photos morph into each other. The room begins to spin.

I need air.

An oversized mirror leans against a wall. I see my reflection. Silent tears roll down my cheeks, but I don't feel them.

I need to leave. My feet start to move, but a photo tucked into the corner of the frame catches my eye and I freeze. Zack and Emily, arms wrapped around each other, smile broadly for the camera. But that's not what has stopped my heart from beating. It's the *lighthouse* they are standing in front of.

No.

Ripping the photo from the frame, I look at their faces one more time.

They're happy.

In love.

The woman's words haunt my ears.

"He was so in love with her, so desperate to keep her with him, he turned to a cheap copy. He doesn't give a damn about you."

I shred the picture to pieces.

It's not enough.

I look around for something. Anything. I grab a shoe and throw it at the mirror, but it doesn't break. So I find something else— a perfume bottle. And this time I wind up before I heave the heavy bottle from my trembling hand. A loud shatter rings through the still room. A hundred tiny pieces of glass fall to the ground. I turn, water still dripping from everywhere on my body, and slowly walk out of the house.

Nikki

I wake to the sound of the engine humming. The vibration coming from below leaves a constant shake that's not quite enough to rock me back to sleep, but the perfect amount to make me queasy. My neck aches from sleeping scrunched up in the cramped seat, but I guess I shouldn't complain since the bus is nearly full and I had two seats to stretch out onto.

I sit up, looking out the tall Plexiglas window and watch the endless miles of desert pass for a while. It's barren and bleak, much like I feel. Only four hours of the twenty-hour bus trip has passed. Six more till we change at the New Mexico border. The older woman who sat next to me at the bus station last night smiles and offers me a bottle of water.

"Thanks." I take it, having brought none of my own supplies. It's not really like it was a planned trip.

"Where are you heading?" she asks.

"Texas."

"Vacation?"

I think about it for a moment before responding. "No. Heading home." My voice is glum.

She nods. "Well, I'm on my way to New Mexico. My sister passed away."

"I'm sorry to hear that."

"Didn't really like her much, but thank you all the same." She smiles warmly at me. "You seem sad, everything okay?"

"Yeah. Well, not really. But it will be when I get back home."

"Home is a place we either love or dread going back to," she offers. "I'm glad yours sounds like a place you love."

"Is yours a place you dread?" I ask curiously. Based on what she's already revealed about her sister, it definitely doesn't sound like a place she loves.

"Yep. Been dreading going back for thirty years."

"You haven't been back home in that long?"

"Nope. Went back once after I moved away. It just didn't feel like home anymore. Too many bad memories."

I swallow down the memory of yesterday, thinking how a place I'd quickly grown to love, a place that actually felt like home, had come to feel like an imposter in only a few short hours. I nod at her, trying to be polite, but no longer wanting to talk. She takes the hint and falls asleep not long after.

Ashley and I text back and forth to help pass the time. She's in class, but that doesn't stop her from responding instantaneously. I'm not sure where I would be right now if I didn't have her. The minute she heard my voice yesterday, she knew it wasn't good news. She had no idea just how bad it was. The shock still hasn't worn off for me. I'm afraid, once it does, I won't be able to breathe again.

After a three-hour delay at the next station, my last bus finally pulls up. The line to board is shorter than the last, and I'm grateful it looks like I'll get a seat to myself again. I've done nothing but sit for a full day, yet I'm more exhausted than I've ever been in my life.

I doze off a few minutes after we pass the *Welcome to New Mexico* sign, my brain replaying yesterday morning over and over in my head until the record is finally worn out. Dreams take over where my conscious state leaves off.

I'm four or maybe five years old and the man comes to visit me again. He comes every few weeks. He only stays an hour or two but we always have fun. Sometimes he takes me for ice cream, other times, like today, we go to the park. He pushes me on the swing high. Really high. Mom's too afraid to let me soar through the air, she thinks I'm too little. But I'm not. I'm big and Mike doesn't treat me like a baby.

After the park we go out for hamburgers. To a real restaurant, not the kind where you carry your food on a tray to the table yourself. The kind where someone else carries the tray for you. He tells me to put the white cloth napkin on my lap and smiles when I do.

"How has Mom been lately?" he asks. He always asks weird questions about Mom.

"She's good. She's been tired a lot lately. Sometimes it's hard for her to get out of bed. But I can make toast for us," I declare proudly.

"Do you cook anything else?"

"Sure. I cook eggs and chicken nuggets and spaghetti."

"You use the top of the stove and the inside?"

"You mean the oven?"

He grins. "Yes, I mean the oven. Where is Mom when you're cooking?"

"Sometimes she's in bed. I told you she's tired a lot lately. The Doctor gave her some new medicine. I have to bring it to her at 8, 12, 4, and again before I go to bed."

"So you also dispense Mom's medicine."

"Dispense?" I crinkle up my nose like something smells bad.

"It means to give out."

Oh. Then yes. I nod. He always asks so many questions. But he asks them fast, one right after the other, so it feels more like we're playing a game. He smiles when I get some right. I like when he smiles. He doesn't do it very much. He and Mom fight a lot when he comes to pick me up. Then he's in a bad mood. They fight more when he drives me home too. I don't think Mom likes him very much. But Mike loves Mom, he says so every time before he leaves.

"Do you have any friends, Nicole?"

"Not really," I say feeling badly. I don't want to disappoint him, but there isn't much time for friends with Mom being sick lately.

"Wouldn't it be nice to have a sister?"

I nod briskly. I'd love to have a sister. Then I could play all day and still keep watch on Mom.

Mike's quiet on the ride back home. We pull into the driveway, he gives me a kiss on the forehead and pulls a flower out of the back seat like he always does. A purple lily. I run into my room as soon as I get in like I always do. I throw away the old lily and put in the new one. I keep it there until the next time he comes. It gets all shrively, but he always comes before it's completely dead.

I hear them fighting a minute later. Mike yells something about his daughters. It sounds like he really wants to spend more time with them. I hope that doesn't mean he won't come visit anymore. He's nice to me and takes me out. Mom doesn't go out much anymore.

The fight gets louder and Mom screams at him to leave. She sounds pretty upset. I listen with my ear pressed to the door until the door slams and the car pulls out of the driveway. Then I go to check on Mom, like I always do.

"Mom? What are you doing?"

She's shoving things into a garbage bag frantically. "We have to move tomorrow," she says with that look I see on her face a lot lately.

I really don't want to move again, it feels like we just got here. I like this place. There are even a few kids that live close by. I was hoping maybe I could even make some friends. But Mom looks upset. I hate to see her that way. "Okay Mommy." I walk to where she is sitting on the floor, shoving things from the bottom drawer into the bag. I take the bag from her hands. "Did you remember to take your medicine at four?" I ask.

She shakes her head. "Go back to bed. I'll bring it to you and then I'll pack the boxes for us."

The bus grinds to an abrupt halt. My eyes dart open. I suddenly feel sick. I rush to the back of the bus and open the bathroom door, thank god it's empty. I vomit before I even have a chance to slide the latch on the door to lock it.

Memories surge back to me like a dam that has been holding back a violent flood. It breaks, sucking me under so deep it's hard to breathe. Memories of Mike. The picture of him clear as day for the first time with my eyes wide open. Mike...Dr. Michael Bennett...Emily's father. All those family photos of him on Emily's wall. He used to come visit me. Take me out to play. I was little, but I remember now. Why didn't I remember before? Why didn't he ever tell me he was my father?

I remember the day I threw out the last lily. It was shriveled and black, pieces flaked off of it when I touched it. Why did he stop coming to see me? What did I do wrong?

It's impossible to fall asleep during the rest of the bus ride. Nine hours go by, things pass by outside my window, but it's all a blur. Nothing makes sense. It's all too much to be a coincidence.

I replay Mrs. Bennett grabbing my arm that day when I ran out of Zack's house. She demanded to know what I was doing there. Did she know who I was? Did Zack know who I was the whole time too?

I agonize over the unknown every minute of every hour of the remaining trip. In the end, the only thing that I'm sure of is that my heart is broken.

Chapter 39

Zack

She never showed up for school, or for our date. At first I thought maybe she was scared. Afraid to go through with what we had planned for last night. But she didn't answer my calls or my texts, so eventually I went to her Aunt's house. She looked upset, but said Nikki had found out some information about her Mom that morning and probably needed some alone time.

I remember needing time away from everyone and everything after Emily died, wanting to take a time out from the world. So I went back home. I was upset she didn't come to me; I would have helped her. Or even just held her if that's what she needed. We didn't have to go through with our plans.

But now it's morning and I still haven't heard from her and my worry has turned to panic. What the hell is going on? So I'm back at her Aunt's house at six am. I just want to know she's home and safe. She doesn't even need to talk to me.

I ring the bell twice but no one answers. There's a hollow feeling in the pit of my stomach and every minute that passes I know something is really wrong. Her Aunt's car is in the driveway, so I know she's home. I wait a few minutes to give her time—

maybe she needs to get dressed and get to the door. But no one comes. My heart beats so loudly with anticipation, I feel like it might come through the wall of my chest. I wait more, still no one comes. So I start banging. Pounding so hard the door begins to loosen from the hinges. Still no answer. So I start yelling. "Open up the door! Open up the goddamn door!" Two neighbors come out in robes before the door finally opens.

Aunt Claire's face is swollen like she's been crying and she steps aside and motions for me to come in.

"Where is Nikki?" I demand, heading down the hall to her room before she has time to respond. I swallow hard finding it empty. Something deep inside of me knew it would be.

"Where is she?" I scream. Aunt Claire's shoulders jump from the anger in my voice and tears start flowing down her cheeks. I rake my hands through my hair, tugging harshly at the roots.

"I'm sorry. I didn't mean to scare you. But where is she? Is she okay?" Anger and panic twist a knot in my stomach, leaving me feeling like I might be sick. If anything has happened to Nikki I don't know what I'll do. Fuck, I love that girl. More than anything. Please God, let her be okay.

"Sit. Zack. I'll put on some coffee. We need to talk."

An hour later my mind is still racing. I'm not sure what emotions I feel. I'm....numb; in shock, undoubtedly. "Why didn't you tell her yourself?"

"I don't know. I've been asking myself the same question over and over for the last twenty-four hours. Why did I let it come from some woman she doesn't know in a cold government office?" She buries her face in her hands. "When she moved in, I thought she was fragile, I wasn't sure she could handle anything more. She was so close to her Mother, I didn't want to spoil the memories she was trying to find a place for in her heart with secrets."

"She isn't fragile," I tell her, defensiveness in my tone.

"I know that now. Once I got to know her…really know her…I realized that. She's probably the strongest person I've ever met."

"And why didn't you tell her then?"

"Because by then she had found some happiness." She pauses. "She found *you*, Zack. And I was afraid of what telling her would do to both of you. You've both been through so much."

"Does Dr. Bennett know she was living here?" So many random questions whirl through my mind. I'm not sure why I ask, but I suddenly remember Nikki's reaction to seeing him the first time in my yard. She recognized him, but wasn't sure who he was.

"He does now. I went to talk to him at the hospital last night when Nikki didn't come home. He's upset. It's complicated. He was Nikki's mother's doctor and she was very young. But he loved her. He wanted to be with her and his girls. But my sister's disease made her irrational. She wouldn't even let him help. When she stopped taking her medications, she really believed he was going to steal Nikki. He did the best he could with Nikki. It was all she would allow him to do."

"Was he married to Mrs. Bennett when he and Nikki's mother were together?"

"Yes."

"Does Mrs. Bennett know Emily has a sister?"

"She does. She hated my sister. I'm glad she never got to meet Nikki, she would have filled her head with vile things about my sister," she says remorsefully.

It's just so much to take in at once. I need to clear my head, figure this all out. I stand to leave. "You're sure she's safe in Texas?"

She nods. "Her friend Ashley promised she'd keep in touch. She won't tell me much, only that she's upset. But at least I know she's safe."

"Are you going to call the police?"

"There's not much they can do. She's eighteen now."

"When did she…" I remember I don't need to ask her birthday. I already know. It's the same as Emily's.

I walk to the door, and turn back with one last question, even though I know she doesn't have the answer. "Why didn't she come to me?

Mom opens the front door before I can even turn the key.

"Zack, I've been trying to call you."

"What's wrong, Mom?" She has that worried face I've come to dread.

"Dr. Bennett is here."

"Here?"

"Yes. He wants to speak to you."

I walk into the kitchen and find Dr. Bennett waiting. He looks anxious. Seeing him makes me angry.

"What do you want?" I seethe.

"Zack!" Mom's appalled.

"It's okay, Jane. Zack's upset and he has every right to be."

Mom looks between me and Dr. Bennett. Neither of us offers anything more. She takes the hint. "I'll leave the two of you alone to talk." She turns to me. "I'll be upstairs if you need anything."

I nod.

"You've spoken to Claire, I see."

"I shouldn't have had to."

"It's complicated, Zack."

"Why do adults think everything is so complicated? You took advantage of Nikki's mother and kept Nikki in the dark about having a sister. A *twin* sister."

"I'm not proud of what I did. But I loved Nikki's mother."

"Did Emily know?"

"No."

"Why didn't you tell them?"

"It's compli..." Dr. Bennett thinks better of his response when he sees my face.

"It wasn't just the girls I needed to think about, Zack. Mrs. Bennett and Nikki's mom had to be considered too.

"So you kept it a secret for your wife? I'm sure Mrs. Bennett was very concerned what other people would think." My voice is laced with disdain. Not only for Dr. Bennett's actions, but for Mrs. Bennett too. I never really cared for her much. All of the insecurities and materialism that weighed heavily on Emily were bred from her mother.

Dr. Bennett sighs. He's smart. Knows there is no answer that will satisfy me.

"What did you come here for?" I ask impatiently.

"I need to ask you if you were in Emily's room today?"

"What? No." I pause. "I haven't been in Emily's room since before she..."

"Someone was in her room."

"What are you talking about?"

"I came home to find her mirror broken."

"Maybe it just fell over. That thing wasn't even secured to the wall."

"The patio door was wide open and a picture was ripped up next to the shards of glass."

"What picture?"

"It was a picture of you and Emily. The one she kept on her mirror."

I run through a visual slide show in my head. She had so many pictures, I can't recall which was on the mirror. "Which picture was it?"

"You were on that 10th grade class trip up North to Angel's Gate. You were standing in front of the lighthouse."

I've been running for hours.

I'm lost, even though I know exactly where I am.

Grey clouds hang low in the sky mimicking how I feel.

Exhausted by emotion, my eyes sting from tears that never seem to run low.

A thousand thoughts race through my mind as I run.

I try to chase them away.

But the faster I run the faster they come.

So I try harder.

Each footstep reaches the pavement faster than the last.

The burn in my calves travels up through my legs but I keep going.

Faster and faster.

Desperate to chase away my thoughts.

My hands begin to shake.

My body begins to shake.

Eventually my legs give out and I fall to the ground.

Everything changes from warp speed to slow motion.

My body crashes against the concrete.

The momentum from the speed of my fall opens the skin on my knees, my elbow, my arms, my chin.

The pain feels good.

It drains the energy from my mind and finally, at least for a moment, I stop thinking.

Chapter 40

Nikki—

Brookside, Texas

"I totally don't get the fascination," Ashley shrugs as we settle in fifty feet up on top of the Brookside water tower. "Plus this thing is so rusted, I feel like we might fall over any second."

"Look around, isn't it beautiful?" I ask as I point down to the barren, sun burnt field, the sun beginning to set off in the distance.

"Honestly? I find it kind of creepy up here."

"Creepy? What could be creepy about it?"

"I don't know. It just feels sort of…" She struggles to find the right word. "Lonely."

Maybe Ashley's just picking up the vibe from me. Because that's exactly how I've felt the last few days. Lonely. Even though Ashley's been with me since I arrived back in Texas, sadness and loneliness consume me.

"How could you feel lonely when I've been such great company?" I bump my shoulder into hers and smile for the first time since I've been back. I've been miserable and we both know it.

"You're kind of a drag," she teases, even though it's the truth.

"I'm sorry."

"Don't be ridiculous. Even though you suck for company, I'd still rather be here with you than back at the trailer park watching my mother's spawn."

"Gee thanks. I'm better than spawn. That makes me feel awesome."

"No problem." She grins.

My cell phone buzzes in my pocket. He's been calling since I left, but I can't bring myself to answer it. It will only make things more difficult.

"Are you ever going to answer it?"

"No."

"Why not?"

"Why would I? Just to hear him say he never really cared about me...that he was only using me to replace her."

"Your Aunt Claire seems to think he genuinely cares about you. He's been to her house a dozen times to try to get my address."

"Why should I trust anything Aunt Claire says? She knew *everything*. Can you please stop answering the phone when she calls?"

"Fine," she huffs.

"Plus, Aunt Claire doesn't know half the stuff that Zack pulled. If she did, she wouldn't believe Zack was so genuine."

"What doesn't she know?"

"Emily's mother *told me* that he knew. She didn't beat around the bush. She flat out told me he was using me to replace her daughter. She's known him since he was little. We used to run together. He ran with Emily all the time. It was their thing. He took her to lighthouses.

"I guess. But you were twins, Nikki. Is it that odd that you might both like to run and go to lighthouses?" Ashley shrugs.

"He lied to my face. He told me he used to pass by the lighthouses all the time and never even noticed them until he met me. There was a picture of Emily and Zack standing in front of a lighthouse in Emily's bedroom. And when we met Dr. Bennett at the hospital, he lied again. He told me Dr. Bennett was a family friend. Why else would he lie?"

"I don't know. But something just seems off."

"Whose side are you on? I didn't even think you liked Zack?"

"I'm always on your side. I was worried he would hurt you."

"Looks like you had good reason to worry."

She sighs. "Alright. I'm not gonna win this argument. So I'll just go with I told you so. You don't have to ask me twice. It's so rare I'm the one in the right with our history." She grins.

"Thanks. That makes me feel better." I force a smile. "You know what else is screwed up?"

"There's more?" she teases.

"I lost a sister, and yet I'm grieving more over Zack."

"You never really had a sister to lose."

"I never really had Zack to lose either."

We sit in comfortable silence until it's dark.

"Ready to go, Ms. Kunas?"

"I don't think you can keep calling me celebrity names if I don't live in California anymore."

"So you're staying in Texas for good?"

"You're all I have," I say with sarcasm, although it's the truth.

"That's pretty sad." Ashley smiles and gets up, offering me her hand. "Come on, let's get down from this depressing place.

Nikki—

Four days later

"You've looked at the phone sixty three times in the last hour," Ashley plops down on the couch next to me. Her tone lets me know she has just slightly less patience about my obsessive phone checking than when I got here.

"You've been counting the times I check my phone?" I use sarcasm to gloss over the fact that I really am consumed with checking it lately.

"So, let me get this straight. You want him to call so you can *not* pick up the phone? I just want to get inside your head and figure out what the hell is going on in there."

"He hasn't even called once in the last two days," I say despondently. Ashley is a great friend but nobody could take the mood I've been in for the last few days.

"Maybe it's because you didn't answer his 987 calls the first two days you were here. Did you ever think of that? Maybe he got the message and gets that you don't want to talk to him. Or do you?"

Ashley means well. I know it doesn't make sense, but I don't want to talk to Zack and yet I don't want him to stop calling either. Rather than explain, I change the subject. "I'm going to Kroger's this week to see if I can get my old job back."

"Do you really intend to drop out of school and get a GED? You were the best student at Brookside before you left," Ashley chides. We seem to have switched roles lately. It hasn't taken her long to get comfortable in her new motherly lecturing tone.

"I need to save for my own place, Ash." I've been back in Texas four days and Ashley's mom has mentioned how cramped the trailer is a few times already. Pawning the sapphire ring my aunt gave me paid for the bus tickets, and I still have some money left over, but it's definitely not enough to move on my own.

I don't think I'll ever get over the guilt of selling a ring that was once my grandmother's. I have so few memories of Mom smiling. The ring had given me visions of a young Mom and Aunt Claire laughing together as they played dress up, pretending to be princesses.

I need to clear my head. "I'm going to go for a run. Wanna come?"

"Run?" She looks me at me like I'm crazy. "I wouldn't even walk if I had a choice."

I didn't tell Ashley my run was going to lead to the cemetery, I've been depressing enough the last few days. Since I arrived back in Texas, all I've wanted to do was go see Mom. I only wish it wasn't a headstone I was going to see.

The only indication of Mom's plot is a simple slate gravesite marker, so different than the ornate headstone that marks my sister's grave. It's been a long time since I've been here, the dirt I left behind has turned to green grass. Her site looks just like everyone else's around here now. It sort of makes me feel bad that there's nothing to make her spot stand out.

I sit for a while, thinking about how much my life has changed since the last time I was here. I was sad that day too. "I miss you, Mom," I whisper. "At least Emily has you." A tear runs down my cheek. "How come I'm the one that got left behind?

Chapter 42

Zack—

Two days later

"My ass is numb," Keller shifts in his seat in the front of the Charger.

"It matches your brain then," I retort quickly.

"How much longer we have to go?" he asks.

"You're worse than a five year old."

He shrugs and begins to entertain himself by tossing jellybeans in the air and trying to catch them in his mouth. My floor is covered with all his misses.

"So what's the chick's name we're meeting again?"

Seriously? I just said her name ten minutes ago. "Ashley. Her name is Ashley."

"Is she hot?"

"I have no idea. I've never met her. You know all this already, bonehead."

"I forgot. How's her voice at least?"

"I don't know. Fine I guess." I concentrate on the never-ending road in front of me. We've been on the road for eighteen hours, not counting the six hours we stopped at some flea bag motel to crash for a while last night.

"She better be hot since I agreed to come all this way with you," he warns, tossing a purple jellybean in the air that hits him in the nose before bouncing to the floor.

"You didn't agree to come. Because I didn't invite you."

"I'm here aren't I?"

"Because you showed up at my house at the time you knew I was leaving and yelled road trip."

"Yeah, so I agreed to come."

"Whatever." I shake my head. There's no point in trying to explain the difference to Keller. I'm actually grateful to have the company. The trip has been long and boring, my eyes getting heavy behind the wheel on more than one occasion.

My heart rate speeds up as we pass a sign that reads *Welcome to Texas*. I can't wait to see her. It's been torture for the past week. I was climbing the walls when Ashley finally called me yesterday.

"Did you know Emily was Nikki's sister?" she asked the minute I picked up the phone.

"No!" I exclaimed. "And who the hell is this?"

"It's Ashley. I'm …"

"I know who you are."

"You do?"

"Yeah. Nikki talked about you all the time. Are you with her?"

"Yes. Well, not right this minute. She's out running. Again."

"Is she okay?"

"No. She's a puddle."

"A puddle?" I inquired, not understating the term.

"You know. Cries all the time. I don't have long. She's like my shadow lately…I'm sure she'll be back in a few minutes."

"Where are you?"

"We're back at my house. She's decided she's dropping out of school and starting a supermarket career at Kroger's since you've stopped calling her because you only really loved her sister. She thinks you were trying to replace Emily with the closest copy you could find. Are you?"

My heart squeezes in my chest. "Of course not. I love her, Ashley."

"Well, when you stopped calling nineteen times a day she kind of assumed you didn't. Know what I mean?"

"Her Aunt and my mother told me to give her space. They said she needed to process it all and that I was just pushing her too fast." Damn I'll never listen to anyone again. My gut told me they were wrong, that I needed to keep after her. I thought giving her space would only make her fill in the missing pieces with things that didn't exist. I wasn't wrong.

"Well her Aunt and your Mother got it ass backwards. She's gone from depressed to angry. You may want to be prepared if you come. She's probably going to unload on you," Ashley warns.

"Thanks, but I can handle it. I'm leaving in the morning," I told Ashley— no thinking about it and no waiting. I'm done following every else's stupid advice.

"I told her we would go back to the depressing water tower she likes so much tomorrow. She thinks it heals her or some stupid crap like that," Ashley snapped and I understood why Nikki likes her so much— straight shooter. Not much of a filter.

"Where's the depressing water tower. That's where I'll head," I said, not giving her an option.

"It's in Brookside."

"Give me the address."

I'm still shocked that she did. My parents weren't exactly happy I was skipping out of school and driving a quarter of the way across the country, but they really didn't object too strenuously. My guess is they knew I was going no matter what they threatened.

255

We arrive right on time at the water tower where Ashley told us to meet her.

Keller gets out of the car with me. "You're staying down here," I say. "Wait a little bit to see if her friend Ashley is with her, I'll send her down to you if she is. Either way, take the car and go find us a hotel for tonight."

"I can drive the Charger?" Keller's eyes light up like a kid on Christmas morning.

"Be careful with her." I toss him the keys.

"I will." He grins widely. There's no way he's not opening it up full throttle the minute he gets out of the parking lot, but I could care less. There's one thing on my mind and that's getting to Nikki.

I'm not even slightly winded when I make it to the top of the fifty-three-stair climb. My entire body is fueled with adrenaline; I could run up Mt. Kilimanjaro if it meant getting to see Nikki at the top.

I walk the narrow catwalk to the other side of the wide tower. Not surprisingly, they're the only two up here. Ashley stands, clearing the view to Nikki who looks up to see where her friend is going at the same minute I catch sight of her. It knocks the wind right out of me.

I'm angry. I'm relieved. I'm so jumbled and filled with mixed emotions, I'm not sure whether to scream at her for leaving or to grab her and never let her go. The one thing I am absolutely, positively sure of in this moment is that I fucking love this girl. With everything I have. She's in my heart and soul. Never in my life have I ever felt so strongly about anything. It almost feels as if my whole life has been a series of tests, just so I could get the answers wrong and know when it's finally right.

Ashley smiles wearily, nods and slips past me wordlessly, quickly making her way down the stairs. Nikki and I hold each other's gaze for a long moment. I see pain and sorrow in her eyes that almost makes me break right on the spot.

I approach her slowly, bending at the knees so we're eye level. I feel like my heart is completely exposed and she can either chose to take it or to break it into a million little pieces. Looking at her, one thing's for certain: if she takes it, I'll never get it back. But she's worth the chance of putting it all out there.

"Hi," I say quietly.

"Hi." she whispers back. Her blue-green eyes flicker with what I think is hope. I move in closer. She looks away, unable to hold the intensity of my stare. Gently, I cup her cheek and force her gaze back to me.

"I don't understand." She pauses. "What are you doing here?"

"I came for you."

"Why?" she hesitates, her eyes darting from mine.

"You have to ask why I came for you? Don't you know how I feel about you?"

"I thought I knew."

"How I feel about you hasn't changed. Except maybe my feelings have grown stronger."

"Really? Do you always lie to the people who you feel strongly about?"

"I didn't lie."

"You told me you barely remembered even passing lighthouses. That they were our special place. I *saw* the picture of you and Emily on her mirror, Zack."

"It was a school trip in tenth grade. We went on a boat ride around the harbor. I didn't even remember there was a lighthouse there."

"And Dr. Bennett at the hospital? He's just a family friend?"

I blow out a breath. "I'm sorry. I had no idea he was your father. I swear. You had just found out you couldn't find out about your sister for a few months. You were disappointed. Upset. I didn't want to make it worse." I pause. "I know it's a stretch, but he is a family friend. He's been our neighbor for ten years."

"But why would Mrs. Bennett tell me you knew, if you didn't?"

"I know she found you at the cemetery and what she said to you. Dr. Bennett found out and told me. He's devastated you found out this way. She just wanted you out of town. She was worried people would find out her husband had an affair. But he's not like her, Nikki. Not at all. He loved your mother and he loves you. She's a bitter person. My mother told me Dr. Bennett moved out of the house last night. I guess it took this to make him see how bad it really was."

She's scared, I see it in her eyes. They warm when they meet mine, but she quickly withdraws. "Do you wish I was Emily when you're with me, Zack?"

I wince. Hearing her ask the question causes me physical pain. "I've never wished anything, when I was with you except for time to stand still."

She eyes me wearily.

"I don't understand why this was our path, but I know fate brought us together." I say without wavering.

Nikki's face softens. Our eyes meet, but she quickly looks away again.

"Look at me." Her eyes jump back to mine. "I'm in love with you." Our gaze finally locks. I brush the hair behind her ear and cup both her cheeks in my hands. "When you're not around, I'm lonely in a room full of people." I pause. "Everything is better with you. *I'm* better with you."

A tear rolls down her cheek.

"No crying." I wipe it away with my thumb.

She hesitates, but smiles a little.

"God, I missed that smile." I look down at her lips.

She smiles a little wider.

"I missed those lips too." With all her sexy curves, it's the curve of her mouth into a smile that does me in.

Nikki

His mouth crushes against mine, the intensity and rawness of the kiss jarring me at first, but I quickly melt into him. I'm breathless by the time he pulls his head back. But I fall hard, losing everything else around us, when he kisses me again, this time beautifully gentle. Our eyes locked, he gazes at me as he worships my mouth with feather-light kisses from one corner all the way around and back again. Then he kisses me so deeply, so full of emotion that he steals my heart along with my breath.

We stay that way for a long time. Stealing kisses and smiles, as the daylight turns to darkness and the moon shines brightly over us. "I almost forgot." Zack reaches into his pocket and pulls out a box. "Happy Valentine's Day."

A beautiful antique heart locket. Zack opens it for me. "I thought maybe you could put a picture of your Mom on one side and you on the other, so you're always next to each other." He smiles.

"I'd love that. Thank you."

There's an inscription on the back, but it's too dark and I can't make out the words. "I can't read it," I say in a soft voice. "What does it say?"

Zack stares at me. I see his throat work to swallow before he speaks. "It says love needs no words. You had me before you even spoke." He pauses, slipping the chain over my neck. "Now you have both my hearts."

Tears stream down my cheeks. He wipes them away. "Can you please not cry."

"But they're good tears, not bad tears."

"Still. It kills me to see any tears on your beautiful face."

I smile. He lifts the locket from between my cleavage. "I like where it falls," he grins devilishly while fingering the heart on the chain where it dangles.

"I have another present."

"Another one?"

He reaches into his other pocket and pulls out something. "Happy Birthday."

"Is that...?"

"Yes." He smiles. "Oh my god. How did you know where to find it?"

"Ashley mentioned you sold a ring your Aunt gave you. So I made your Aunt go to every pawn store in the area to help me find it."

My Aunt. I feel badly for disappearing on her, even though she kept so many secrets from me. "How is Aunt Claire?" I ask.

"Worried about you. She's really pretty broken up over you finding out and her not being the one to tell you."

"She could have told me herself."

"I know." He kisses me gently on the lips. "It doesn't mean she doesn't love you and hasn't been worried. She needs to explain it to you herself, but she was trying to protect you."

The sunlight gone, a northeast wind blows strong at the top of the tower. The breeze makes me shiver. "Come on. Let's get out of here. I'll call Keller to come get us."

"Keller?"

"Yeah. He decided I invited him on this road trip."

"Did you?"

"No."

We both laugh. As we turn to descend the narrow steps, Zack slips a folded piece of paper into my hand as he takes it. Today I don't wait to read it until he leaves. I stop and open it smiling up at him. *I missed you.* Looking deep into his eyes, I tell him, "I missed you too."

Chapter 44

Nikki

Zack wasn't ready to turn around and drive the twenty hours back to California and we needed some time alone. So we decided to stay in Texas a few more nights. In the end, I spoke to Aunt Claire and decided to go back to California to live with her. Texas wasn't my home anymore, no matter how hard I wanted it to be before Zack showed up.

So tomorrow we're leaving. Oddly, Keller and Ash have hit it off pretty good. I never would have guessed the two of them would like each other. But there's something more than friends brewing between them. We're already planning on her coming out to California this summer.

That brings us to tonight. Zack rented rooms for Ashley and Keller so we can be alone finally. I'm more ready to be with him than I ever was and my heart swells with a heady combination of love and lust as he walks toward the bed from the bathroom. He's wearing skin hugging grey boxer briefs and I can tell he's just as ready.

"I like you in my t-shirt," he says with a wicked grin, reaching for my locket. It's become his new toy; he seems to need to touch it multiple times a day. He doesn't even pretend it has anything to do with jewelry anymore. He trails his knuckles up and down my breasts, the locket dangling in the palm of his hand. "I like you out of my shirt even better." He reaches for the hem of his t-shirt and lifts it up and over my head.

The room is still and I can hear his breath speed up when he sees me in my pink lacey bra and panties. We've fooled around before. A lot. We've even seen each other fully naked. But tonight is different and we both know it. Everything is about to change.

He stands at the edge of the bed looking at me, taking his time to graze his eyes up and down my body. The desire I see makes my body break out in goose-bumps. "Last chance to change your mind," he says, searching my eyes. He wants to be sure I'm ready. I love that about him. Always putting my needs first.

I shake my head and crawl to him at the edge of the bed. He undresses me painstakingly slowly. I'm nervous but I know he likes when I take the lead sometimes, so I pull him to me, covering his mouth with mine, and we both get lost in a kiss that makes me glad I'm not standing. I slip down his underwear and he groans as my hand grazes his hardness.

He centers himself over me, our mouths entwined in a kiss that feels like it would physically hurt to disconnect. He reaches over to the end table and grabs a condom, disconnecting only briefly to put it on. Instinctively, I wrap my legs around him and he pulls his head back. He's positioned perfectly over me but he stills.

He laces our fingers together and lifts our entwined hands over my head. "I know it will feel amazing to be inside you, but that's just a bonus. I need to be inside you so we can be connected even more."

"I want that too," I respond in a whisper. He kisses me gently as he pushes into me slowly. A burst of pain makes me gasp, but the pain eases almost as fast as it hit me. Our mouths find a rhythm that synchronizes with the rock of his hips as he gently pushes in and out. He goes slow, inching his way in a little at a time, until he's fully seated. Settling, he gives me time to adjust to the full but incredibly wonderful feeling of him being inside of me.

Breaking our intense, languid kiss he draws his head back to check on me before moving. "You okay?" he whispers.

I nod.

"You sure?"

"I would be if you would start moving a little." His eyebrows arch in surprise and he lets out a raspy chuckle. But the laughter is quickly replaced by something more sinister. He buries his head into my neck and nips and kisses his way from my collarbone to my ear. His rhythm increases as the gentle kisses turn to sucking and his light nips become more forceful.

My body matches his rhythm, thrust for thrust, and together we rock back and forth, completely and utterly connected in every way. Mind, heart, soul and now body. It's beautiful and breathtaking and the only thing I regret is not being able to see every inch of us joined as we become one for the first time.

A small moan escapes my lips and it ratchets up both our needs even more. I feel his sweat-slick body tense and I know he must be close. He pulls his head back, his face filled with so much need, but again he stops to put me first. "I love you, Nikki." His voice is raw and intense and any doubt I had left is erased. My eyes fill with tears of happiness.

"I love you, too."

He swivels his hips a little and his body finds a new way to pleasure mine that I didn't even know was possible. My breathing hitches, my eyes roll into the back of my head and shudders rack through me.

"So beautiful," he whispers, his eyes keenly focused on watching me give whatever is left over to him. He pumps into me hard a few more times; the groan coming from deep in his throat is the sexiest sound I've ever heard.

Even as we slow our rhythm and eventually stop, he still kisses me with more passion than I ever imagined could be real.

We spend hours exploring, learning each other's bodies, until we finally pass out from exhaustion. The last thing I remember is feeling like I'm home again. I always knew home wasn't a place, I just didn't know I could find it with a person who would be so deeply raveled in my life before we ever met.

Epilogue

Nikki—

Valentine's Day— 3 years later

I wake to Zack's grumbling when he trips over a box. Yet again. I smile in the dark as he tries in vain to quietly slip out to his early morning class. Instead, a low string of curses litter the room as he limps toward the bed, muttering something about a broken toe. I don't let on that I'm awake when he leans down and kisses my forehead, slipping something under my pillow.

I wait till I hear the front door close, then slip the note out. He hasn't left me one in a while. Even though I miss getting them, it makes his little vignettes that much more special. I unfold it. *Will you be my Valentine, Birthday Girl?* Like a fourteen-year-old schoolgirl, I hold it against my chest and cherish it for what it is. A note from the cutest boy in school, who I have a mammoth size crush on. Only we're starting our last year of college now.

Two weeks ago, we finally took the plunge and moved in together. A small apartment near campus— the Waldorf, it's not—

269

but I love it as much as if it were some fancy penthouse. It's funny, the last three years we spent four nights a week together, so I didn't think it would feel that different when we actually lived together. Yet it's totally different. And it has nothing to do with Zack not having to sneak out before Aunt Claire gets home either. I'd told him Aunt Claire wouldn't mind, but he insisted on doing it until the day I moved out— he didn't want to rub it in her face that we were sleeping together. Although there is no way that she didn't know.

After I came back from Texas, Aunt Claire and I spent a lot of time talking. I knew before I met her that she was keeping secrets from me, but my heart was still wounded that she didn't tell me about Emily.

I found out she'd stayed in Long Beach her whole life to keep an eye on my sister. And she kept tabs on Mom and I, too. Growing up, I remember we would get these big deliveries once a month — fresh fruit, vegetables, yogurt — I loved the day the delivery man came each month. Mom never mentioned who sent the groceries, I cried for an hour when Aunt Claire told me it was her. For seventeen years she loved me, Mom and Emily from afar — a guardian angel watching over us. Now Aunt Claire and I have each other, and our guardian angels are Mom and Emily.

It didn't take long for me to forgive Aunt Claire for her not telling me about my dad and Emily. She was only trying to protect me. I just needed to see things clearly. These days, I think of her like a best friend. Although I'd never tell Ashley— she still holds a bit of a grudge against Aunt Claire for the things that happened three years ago. That, and Ash would be crushed if she knew that my relationship with Aunt Claire rivaled ours.

And then there's my dad. I kept away from him the first few months I was back in California. It was all too much to deal with. But Zack eventually convinced me to meet Dr. Bennett for lunch one day. I'll never forget walking into the restaurant that Saturday afternoon. I saw him sitting at the table and our eyes locked. He stood and suddenly I was five years old again and he was Mike. If Zack hadn't been standing next to me, I would have fallen on the floor when I saw my dad break down and cry. He handed me a single purple lily before I left that day.

I look over to my nightstand, finding a fresh purple lily. He's brought me one every week since that lunch. Somehow I know I'll always have one. Over the last two and a half years, we've spent a lot of time talking about Mom. He loved her with all his heart, he really did. But it's complicated…

So much has changed over the last three years. I look around the room. It's littered with boxes, but I've made progress. My tan musty cardboard has been upgraded. They're now pretty boxes, colorful shades of pink, courtesy of the Box Store. I like to think they give the apartment a shabby chic look, but I'd venture to guess Zack has other choice words to describe my neurosis. Although he's never complained once about them being all over the place.

Friday is Zack's long day. He's been at school since seven this morning and it's nearly seven in the evening now. I expect him any minute. He's usually wiped out and sore after four classes followed by hours and hours of grueling football practice. But something tells me he'll get a second wind when he gets a look at his Valentine's Day present. My new red nightie, a form fitting halter corset made of gorgeous lace with a satin tie front. It fits like a second skin. Which is good, because second skin matches with all the skin that shows when I turn around; the matching G-string leaves little to the imagination.

Hearing his keys in the door, I open it, knowing his hands will be full with all his equipment. It clanks loudly on the wooden floor when he lets it drop without a word and comes straight for me. Laying my palm to his chest, I stop him before he pounces. I hand him a folded-up note, the first one I've ever given him, and he arches an eyebrow. Neither of us speaks while he unfolds it.

I'll always be your Valentine. Thank you for giving me so much more than I could have imagined. I love you.

He looks up at me, gazing into my soul with his blue eyes that tell me everything I need to hear without saying a word. Scooping me up, he cradles me gently in his arms. So different than how he'd probably planned to have me just moments ago when I opened the door. Tonight is about love. There's a time for crazed and frantic—heck, I love it every way with Zack. But tonight...tonight will be slow and sweet. My favorite.

He walks into the bedroom with me in his arms and stops short, taking in everything that isn't there. The boxes. They're all gone. Every last one of them. When his eyes finally find their way back to mine, I say the words I've waited twenty-one years to feel.

"I'm finally home."

Dear Readers,

Thank you for taking a chance on something different with me! I loved writing Left Behind and getting the opportunity to explore younger characters. It was an incredible experience and one I thoroughly enjoyed co-writing with Dylan Scott!

My next series will be a return to contemporary romance in early 2015. Please take a sneak peek at Throb, coming late January 2015!

Sign up to receive Chapter 1 of Throb!

http://eepurl.com/4nxpP

And please add Throb and Beat to your reading list!

Throb: http://bit.ly/ZyfrmK
Beat: http://bit.ly/1thI45l

Acknowledgements

Thank you to all of the bloggers that take time away from their family and friends to support Indie Authors! Without your help, the Indie community would not have flourished to what it is today.

A special thank you to some amazing ladies that have done so much to help us bring Left Behind to fruition. Nita, Sommer, Lisa, Caitlin, Carmen and Dallison— Thank you for beta reading, editing, making kick-ass trailers, beautiful covers, and letting us drive you nuts with changes!

Thank you to all of the Ashby ladies! Evette, Maya and Jenna— for family beta reading so we could get feedback from two generations of readers! Your opinions and feedback helped to shape the story into what it is today.

Finally, thank you so much to all the readers. We love your notes, emails and reviews! Today, more than ever, you have so many choices and we are thrilled you picked us to spend some time with!

Much love,

Vi & Dylan

Other Books by Vi

Worth the Fight
amzn.com/B00FLG5B9S

Worth the Chance
Amzn.com/B00I2UKQOK

Belong to You
Amzn.com/B00BUTCXLE

Made for You
Amzn.com/B00DPWVKS6

First Thing I See
Amzn.com/B00AWXY3HG

Connect with Vi

http://fb.me/ViKeeland
http://on.fb.me/1uxLPTH
Twitter - @vikeeland
Instagram - @vi_keeland
http://www.vikeeland.com

CPSIA information can be obtained
at www.ICGtesting.com
Printed in the USA
LVHW092356020420
652092LV00007B/1772